My Current Situation

AN ATLANTA TALE

A Romcom Novel by

MARLON
MCCAULSKY

MLM PUBLISHING COMPANY

Atlanta, GA 30349
© Copyright 2019 Marlon McCaulsky
Publishing Copy MLM Publishing Company
Printed in the United States of America

Editor: Cynthia Marie
Cover models:
Chasity Marie as Deja Queen
Aaron Harris as Kurt Bishop
LeThoams Lee as Jason Trammell
Photography by Furery T. Reid Photography
Video photography by Lamont Gant
Makeup by LaCora Monet & Chasity Marie
Typesetting by Marlon McCaulsky
Cover graphic design by Lamont Gant
Back cover graphic design by Marlon McCaulsky
Website designer: Aaron Johnson Sr.
Executive Producers: Marlon McCaulsky & Sheena McCaulsky

Also by Marlon McCaulsky

The Pink Palace

The Pink Palace 2: Money, Power, & Sex

The Pink Palace 3: Malicious

From Vixen 2 Diva

Born Sinners

Used To Temporary Happiness

Returned

A Dangerous Woman

Real Love

If I Was Your Girlfriend: An Atlanta Tale

Anthologies

Blush

Romance For The Streets

Love & Life

The Freak Files Reloaded

Urban Fantasies 1-4 (eBook)

Bad Girl (eBook)

Films

Returned

Temporary Happiness

No Time For Love (short film)

Annulment (short film)

Friends, how many of us have them?

.

 Deja Queen   Kurt Bishop   Jason Trammell

 Danielle Queen   Starr Sales   Rick Westbrook

 Darnell Smith   Kima Rowe-Sales   Mike Sales

MY CURRENT SITUATION BY MARLON MCCAULSKY

Prologue
The Key To A Great Relationship

COLLEGE PARK - RICK & JASON'S APARTMENT

"Remind me again ... what are you getting married for?"

Rick glared at his best friend's reflection in the mirror behind him. The black suit and red tie made Jason Trammell look like a Wall Street stock broker but his perfect hairline, beard, and goatee on his ebony skin exuded black excellence. Jason always thought he was the original playa from the Himalayas. Today, they were in their apartment getting ready to attend Rick's engagement dinner at his mother's house. It was two weeks before his wedding to his college sweetheart, Danielle Queen.

"Because that's what you do when you're in love with a woman," he replied, tying his tie.

"Yeah, yeah, yeah, that notwithstanding, bruh, you are twenty three years old, educated, got reasonably good looks when you're not being compared to me, and you've barely gotten your dick wet. Why do you wanna lock yourself down so soon?"

"Remind me again ... why are we friends?"

"Because your Momma said so," Jason retorted.

Rick rolled his eyes and adjusted his tie. Even though it was a joke there was a bit of truth to it. Rick's mother had been like a second mother to Jason since they were in Kindergarten. They were as close as brothers and had each other's back no matter what.

"Look Rick, Dani is a great girl and all but y'all have only been dating for two years. You just gonna give up your playa card in the prime of your career? And you know she's a control freak."

4

He chuckled. "We've only been a couple for two years but we've known each other since we were kids, you know this," he stressed. "And she's not a control freak."

Jason gave him the side eye. "Really, so she wasn't the one who proposed to you? What's the rush? A four week engagement and then lockdown for life? C'mon son!"

"No, it didn't happen like that and we're not rushing into anything. We discussed it and we both came to the same conclusion that getting married now was the most logical thing for us to do."

Jason stared at his best friend as if he lost his mind. "Wow, so she got you to drink the Kool-Aid, huh?"

"Shut up. We're a modern couple and we have a plan."

"We have a plan," Jason mocked. "We? Don't you mean she has a plan? Because she plans everything. I think she even plans her bowel movements. I mean real talk, I've never once seen her use a public bathroom. Like she just walks around holding that shit in all day. Does she fart around you?"

Rick laughed and looked at his friend. "What the hell kind of question is that? Dani is a classy woman."

"Ok, does she fart around you or not?"

Rick paused briefly then sighed. "Nah, she doesn't."

"What I tell ya bruh!" Jason exclaimed. "I don't trust that shit."

"You don't trust no woman," Rick countered.

"Something ain't right about that." Jason ignored his friend's truth. "Farting is the key to a great relationship. I fart on bitches all the time! Trust me, look that shit up."

Rick shook his head. "I didn't hear you saying all this when Mike and Kima got engaged."

"They've been together since the tenth grade, that shit was inevitable. But you, I know you, you're like me, you a dog. Come on bruh take that damn leash off. Go sniff a bitch or two," Jason said with a shit-eating grin on his face.

Rick sneered at him. "You're a sick man. This is happening, Jay. You need to just accept it."

"Aight, I did my part. Don't say I never tried to help you."

Rick's eyebrows scrunched. "You call this help?"

"Hey, I just want you to be sure about this." Jason straightened his friend's tie. "Cause once you walk down that aisle, ain't no turning back."

Jason walked out of the room and Rick stood there for a second letting Jason's words sink in. As much as a jerk Jason was, he knew he was also in his own way looking out for him. Rick shook his head and left the apartment.

MY CURRENT SITUATION   BY   MARLON MCCAULSKY

Rules Of Engagement

Rick and Jason soon arrived at his mother's house, Ms. Sharon Westbrook. All of Rick's friends called her Ms. Sharon, and as always, she was in the kitchen cooking up something delicious. She was lovingly dubbed as a master southern chef and for tonight's special occasion she made pot roast, greens, roasted potatoes, macaroni and cheese with bacon. Rick gave his mother a kiss on the cheek as she stood over the stove stirring the pot of greens.

"Dang Ms. Sharon," Jason spoke and gave her a kiss, "you done set it off up in here again."

She spotted Rick sticking his finger in the macaroni; and with lightening quick reflexes that defied her age, she swatted his hand away. "Boy, don't put your nasty fingers in there! Other people gotta eat that too."

"Ma, I'm just sampling it for ya!"

"I don't need you to sample nothing, Richard."

"He's so inconsiderate, Ms. Sharon," Jason egged on. "I don't know where he gets his manners from."

Rick glared at his friend. "Really, you of all people are gonna talk about manners?"

"What are you talking about, Richard? Jason has always been a respectable boy."

"Thank you Ms. Sharon."

As soon as she turned her head Jason stuck his tongue out at his friend. He, in return, pretended to scratch his nose with his middle finger. "Anyway, what can I do to help, Mom?"

"You can take out the garbage." She then took a fork and gave Jason a sample of the greens she was keeping warm

8

in the pot. "Try this, baby."

"Aw man! That's delicious!"

"I hate you so much," Rick mumbled and grabbed the trash bag from the can and took it outside. Heading to the curb, he spotted Danielle pulling up to the house. He quickly disposed of the bag then walked toward the car as she parked. Danielle Queen was more than a beautiful young woman. She was everything he wanted. Her black-rimmed glasses sat perfectly on her round face framing her hypnotizing brown eyes. As usual, she wore minimal makeup and her black silky hair was pulled back into a ponytail. Her natural beauty is what always drew Rick to her.

"Hello the future Mrs. Westbrook!" He greeted his fiancé with a passionate kiss.

"How about the future Queen-Westbrook," she corrected with a grin.

"Hey, when you marry a Westbrook you gotta go all the way in."

She pursed her lips. "Did you ever get that tattoo of my name on your chest like you promised you would two years ago?"

His mouth fell open. "Ah … you see what had happened was … ah I'm allergic to ink and I break out into a rash on my left ass cheek and –"

"Shut up!" She laughed. "You're lucky I love you."

"Yes I am."

They started to walk toward the house and she inhaled. "Damn, I can smell your mother's cooking from here."

"Yeah, she done did it again. Jason is already sampling everything."

Danielle let out a slight growl hearing Jason's name. "I bet he is."

They walked inside and Danielle headed toward the kitchen and hugged Ms. Sharon. Danielle was like the daughter she never had but always wanted. She had known

Danielle since she was a little girl in her third grade class with Rick. Over the years she watched them play together, fight each other, and now as she predicted become husband and wife.

"Hello darling!" Sharon greeted her.

"Ms. Sharon," she looked around in awe at the spread, "you have got to teach me to cook like this."

"She doesn't have enough hours in the day to do that," Jason joked.

Danielle narrowed her eyes at him. If Sharon weren't in the room she would have had some very unladylike things to say. They never liked each other much. Jason always thought she was stuck up and Danielle always thought he was a misogynist pig. Only because of their love for Rick they tolerated one another.

"Hello Jason," she greeted dryly.

A pompous smirk spread across his face.

"I'll be happy to teach you, sweetheart."

"Thank you Ms. Sharon." She looked at Rick. "What time is everybody supposed to be here?"

He looked at his watch. "In about a half hour."

"You all go on now." Ms. Sharon shoo'd them out of the kitchen. "I'll have dinner on the table by the time your friends get here."

They all headed toward the living room and just then Jason's phone chirped. He looked at the incoming text and smiled.

"Yeeeah ... I knew she would hit me back!"

Rick looked at his friend. "Who?"

"That cute ass chick we saw working at Kilwin's in Atlantic Station. You know the one with the fat ass that you said could stunt double for Nicki Minaj."

Rick sighed and Danielle frowned at his lie. Jason glanced at them both and grinned. "I'm just fucking with you. I'ma go hit this chick back."

They watched him head outside to make his booty

call.

"And you wonder why I don't like his ass," Danielle reminded.

"Jason's a fool. He just does that to get on your nerves. Don't pay him any attention."

"I never do. You know he can never be allowed to influence our kids."

An apprehensive expression washed over his face. "Kids, as in plural? We, we never really talked about kids."

"No, I guess not," she shrugged, "but our honeymoon will be a great time to start. No more condoms," she sang.

Rick forced a smile. "Whoop whoop."

"I can take time off while you work. Mr. Gant assured me I will have a position at the law firm when I'm ready to return. So, I figure two girls and boy over a five year period would be good. Hopefully we'll luck up and get twins."

"Wow twins … you've given this a lot of thought huh?"

"Of course. We gotta have a plan, right?" She stared at him.

"You're right, three kids, two girls, huh? Maybe twins?"

"Yep. I have a list of names I wanna go over with you later."

"A list?"

"Yeah, just a little Excel spreadsheet I put together a couple weeks ago. Along with some of the best private schools we can get them in. I wonder if we put their names on the list now we can get them enrolled early? Anyway, once we get back from our honeymoon we can deal with all that." She looked at her watch. "I got just enough time to go freshen up before everybody gets here."

Rick nodded. She gave him a quick kiss and trotted happily upstairs to the bathroom. His head was spinning as he thought about everything Danielle had just said. She had planned out everything. He had barely thought about kids much less names. She had already found schools for them and they weren't even conceived yet. Jason's words to him earlier replayed in his head like it was on auto repeat. *'Once you walk down that aisle … ain't no turning back.'*

A few minutes later, the doorbell rang and Rick greeted the other guests. They headed toward the living room where Danielle had just returned.

"Hey everybody!" She greeted them with hugs and they all got comfortable.

Mike Sales was a six foot four defensive tackle for the Georgia Bulldogs. He's been friends with Rick and Jason since junior high. He was, by nature, a gentle giant. By Mike's side was his fiancé, Kima Rowe, who was also Danielle's best friend. She was tall with an athletic build and loved sports as much as he did. She had always been the voice of reason amongst her friends and everybody came to her for advice. Her charm and sexiness had Mike wrapped around every word that came out of her New Orleans twang. They had been a couple, off and on since tenth grade, and became inseparable in their college years.

Sitting next to Mike and Kima was Kurt Bishop. He was a handsome brother who ladies always compared to Morris Chestnut. In return, his friends always called him "baby chestnut" and that annoyed the hell out of him. He was a close friend of Mike's, as well as Danielle and her sister, Deja. Jason always suspected that he and Danielle were a little too close to be 'just friends'. He called guys like Kurt 'sleepers'. His theory was that Kurt played the part of the 'friend' until the female target had that one moment of emotional vulnerability, then move in on that ass.

Rick; however, had never given Jason's theory much thought and after meeting Kurt he decided he was a good dude. Besides, he trusted Danielle.

"So where's Starr?" Mike asked, looking at his watch. "She's usually here before any of us."

Danielle shrugged. "She's probably with Deja and, as usual, she's late."

Jason returned from his phone call, dapped it up with Mike, hugged Kima and gave Kurt a head nod.

"They'll be here," Kima assured. "Two broke college girls aren't gonna pass on a free meal let alone a home cooked one." She inhaled and her stomach rumbled. "Besides, if they're late that's their loss, I'm hungry!"

"You're always hungry ," Danielle quipped.

"No I'm not ... I just like to eat."

Everybody laughed.

Mike put his arm around his girl. "Hey, it's because of that appetite why a brother be eating so good."

"That's right! I take care of my man." Kima kissed him.

"Speaking of eating good," Kurt chimed in, "let me go check on Ms. Sharon and see how she's doing. See if she needs any ... help."

Danielle shook her head. "I see college girls aren't the only ones interested in a home cooked meal."

Jason watched Kurt closely and smirked slyly. *I bet that's not the only thing he interested in,* he thought to himself. He then glanced at Rick and noticed that he looked a little lost in thought.

"Hey bruh, you alright?"

Rick was startled from his thought. "Yeah." He put his arm around his fiancé. "I'm perfect."

"Yes, we are," she added matter of factly.

Jason looked at the two. "I see."

Ms. Sharon emerged from the kitchen. "Dinner's on the table all."

A few minutes later everybody was seated at the dinner table. Ms. Sharon had outdone herself and prepared everything as if the President and First Lady were her guests.

"No matter how many times I eat your cooking ma," Rick shoveled another forkful of tender pot roast in his mouth, "you always come through."

"Thank you, baby. Pretty soon you're gonna have a new cook in your life." She took Danielle's hand.

Jason snickered which caused Danielle to frown.

"Is something funny, Jason?"

"Nah, I'm just thinking about the last time we all had dinner at your place, yum."

Rick glowered. He knew this was a touchy subject for Danielle.

"I know what you're trying to do Jason; and for the record, everybody knows duck is a little bit chewier than chicken. It takes a sophisticated palette to appreciate the texture and flavor of Duck á l'orange." Danielle looked at Kima. "Isn't that right?"

She stared blankly at her best friend. "Ahhh, yeah so I hear, ah, these greens are delicious Ms. Sharon!"

Danielle cocked her head to the side. "Oh really, Kima?" She looked to her left. "Mike?"

"What was the question again?"

Danielle turned to her friend. "Tell them my duck was good, Kurt."

"Huh?" He quickly put a forkful of macaroni in his mouth and mumbled. Everybody chuckled.

"Et Tu, Kurt." Danielle gave him the evil eye.

"It was the best duck I ever had." Rick quickly spoke up. "And that's all that matters!"

Danielle gleamed. "Thank you, baby."

"You want some more Kool-Aid, Rick?" Jason asked sarcastically.

Rick made a fist as an inaudible threat to his friend as the doorbell rang.

"I'll get it," Danielle offered, looking at her watch. "Twenty minutes late as usual." She got up from the table. "You're late," she scolded, opening the door.

Her younger sister, Deja Queen was with her best friend Starr Sales. The only thing Deja and Danielle had in common was that they shared the same father; outside of that, they were polar opposites. Deja was the petite wild child with a huge personality who always seemed to be the center of attention anywhere she went while Danielle was always the responsible sister who always accomplished the goals she set for herself.

Starr was Mike's little sister and everybody loved her. Her mother named her Starr because she told her as soon as she held her for the first time she lit up her world. She wasn't as outspoken as Deja but she was just as confident. Ever since their father passed away; Mike became very protective of her; overly protective to be more accurate. She felt smothered by his constant meddling especially in her love life. Perhaps that was the reason she and Deja became so close. She had her back when Mike got too nosey.

Deja shrugged her shoulders and walked by her. "We got held up at the store. Sorry."

Starr walked in and gave Danielle a hug. "It's my fault, Dani. I couldn't find the right outfit for tonight."

"Um huh," Danielle hummed, knowing she was lying. She was always punctual for everything.

"Well, dinner is already on the table."

"Good, cuz I'm starving!"

Danielle exhaled and followed them into the dining room. The girls greeted everybody and sat down.

"So where are y'all going tonight?" Danielle asked, getting comfortable again.

"Oh, to this new club up in Decatur," Deja responded.

"Now I know Starr doesn't have class tomorrow but don't you have an Economics class at eight?"

Deja rolled her eyes. "It's amazing how you find time to plan a wedding, intern at a law firm and know the details of my school schedule."

"It's called multi-tasking. If you were more focused you could probably do the same," Danielle informed her. "So you gonna skip class again?"

Deja squinted. "Mom? Is that you? You look so unfamiliar right now."

"I'm just saying, if you focus more on class than partying you'll be better off in the long run."

"And if you focus more on minding your own business you'd be less annoying to be around."

The back and forth between the sisters was nothing new for their friends. Even Ms. Sharon was used to the bickering. She knew they would someday have to make peace with each other but today wasn't the day.

Half the time it was more entertaining than anything but Kurt often cringed at his two friends being so savage toward one another. Seeing the storm brewing between the two, he decided to interject. "Ah ... Mike you see that Falcons game? What's wrong with them boys? They act like they just don't wanna win."

"I'm not even wasting my time watching them fools anymore. I'ma Saints fan now."

"Who dat, who dat, who dat say they gonna bet dem Saints," Kima began to cheer in her deep New Orleans dialect.

"Aw, ain't that cute. Good to see you two on the same team. Always in sync with each other," Jason remarked. "But the thing I've been wanting to ask you and Kima is, how did you y'all get engaged before these two but they're getting married before y'all? I mean they made the announcement a month ago and bam!"

Rick rolled his eyes knowing what he was doing. He just wouldn't let it go even though there was some truth to it.

Mike looked at his fiancé. "Well, we talked about it and just decided to wait till after the NFL draft then we can focus on the wedding."

"That just worked better for us," Kima added. "I'm sure they discussed it and are doing what's best for them too."

Danielle looked at Rick. "Yes, we did."

"Yeah, I'm sure ya did," he thought to himself.

As much as Rick was annoyed by Jason's indirect jab about his engagement he had to admit that Mike and Kima seemed to be more on the same page than he and Danielle were. At times it felt like she was already on the next chapter while he was on the first chapter; or even worse, she was writing the book and he was simply a character. Once again Jason's words tormented him, *"she plans everything."*

As everybody continued eat and enjoy their meal Rick sat frozen in his seat. His mind was racing thinking about how his life was about to change—forever. Suddenly the room felt smaller. All the chatter at the table seemed to become unrecognizable and he felt his temperature rise. Then he heard it, a steady thump that became louder and louder like a crazed drummer playing to his own off kilter beat. It felt like all the blood in his body was rushing to his head. His hands felt clammy. Mouth went dry. At this point he didn't know if he was having a heart attack or a hot flash. Danielle looked at him then took his hand. "Babe?"

He looked at her. "Huh?"

"Are you okay?"

He swallowed hard. "Excuse me."

Rick got up from the table and went upstairs to the bathroom. He stood in front of the mirror and splashed cold water on his face. Repeating this a few more times, his body started to feel normal again. He looked up at his refection and saw Danielle behind him in the doorway.

"What's going on? Are you sick?"

"No … I'm okay."

She moved closer to him. "You sure?"

He looked closely at her. There she was. Everything he ever wanted in a woman but couldn't deny what he was feeling.

"Dani, why are we doing this?"

"Because they're our friends and your mother is a

much better cook than—"

"No." He shook his head. "Not that. Why are we getting married so soon?"

Danielle was perplexed by his question. "Because we want to be together, right?"

"Yeah, I want that too, but why are we in such a rush to do it?"

Danielle sighed. "Okay… okay… I know what this is… you're getting cold feet. It's okay it's natural. You're a man and you feel like your whole world as you know it is coming to an end. But it's not baby, this is only the beginning. We have a plan and if we stick to it—"

"Do you hear yourself right now, Dani? We have plan? No, you have a plan. You have a plan for everything!"

She frowned. "What does that supposed to mean?"

"Dani, up until forty five minutes ago, I didn't even know you wanted kids. You chose their sex, how many in five years and even picked out schools. Hell, you've made spreadsheets! I don't even know if I want to have kids right now."

"Wha … What are you saying?"

"We're just moving so fast, I'm just wondering if we're doing the right thing."

"You don't love me?" She asked with tears forming in her eyes.

"I didn't say that. I love you, but I'm not sure about getting married right now."

"Oh my god!" She spoke through clenched her teeth. "This is because of Jason, isn't it?" Two pooled tears left her eyes and slowly slid downward. "I knew it! He's been planting these seeds in your head against me!"

"No, this has nothing to do with him. This is about us! Why are we moving so damn fast?"

"Rick, we've talked about this and decided now is the right time for us. We're both—"

"No, you talked," he interjected. "I just nodded my head and agreed to it like a dumbass!"

"Really?" She shot back with an attitude and crossed her arms. "Well here's your chance! What do you want?"

He grabbed his face. "I don't know."

She stepped closer to him. "No, you wanted your chance to talk so talk." She pointed her finger at him. "Just make sure you say what you mean and be clear! I don't want you to be a dumbass." She used his words against him.

"I don't wanna marry you!"

Danielle stared at him in shock. Rick knew as soon as the words left his mouth it was mistake. She felt as if Rick had shot her through the heart. She never expected to hear those words come from him.

"Dani, I didn't mean …"

He reached for her but she jerked away from him and quickly exited the bathroom. Rick cursed to himself and followed her.

"Dani wait!"

She stormed down the stairs and saw that everyone was gathered together at the bottom of the staircase.

"Is everything ok, sweetheart?" Ms. Sharon asked with concern.

Danielle paused and looked at everybody. "The wedding is off." She grabbed her bag and rushed toward the front door. Rick dashed down the stairs and all eyes focused on him.

"What the hell did you do?" Kurt spoke up.

Rick ignored him and rushed out the door. "Dani, wait up! Please, I didn't mean it!"

Everybody followed them outside, totally baffled as to what they were witnessing. They had never seen Rick and Danielle like this before. Jason; however, realized that his words of caution had gotten through to his friend.

Danielle ignored Rick's pleas and attempted to get into her car.

He grabbed her arm.

"Let me go, Rick!"

"Not until you listen to me!"

"I did! Now, let me go!"

"Yo, you heard her!"

Rick quickly turned around and was agitated seeing Kurt stepping toward him. "Get your own woman, bitch!"

Instantly, Kurt's fist tagged his Rick's jaw sending him to the ground.

"Who's a bitch now, bitch!" Kurt bellowed as Rick writhed on the ground in pain.

Danielle looked at him for a second, got inside of her car and pulled off. Kurt went to his car and left

"Damn." Jason said out loud and gave Rick a helping hand. He wasn't expecting what he saw. "You okay?"

Rick rubbed his face and watched Danielle's car speed down the street. He knew in his heart he wasn't ready to get married but he totally handled the situation the wrong way. One thing was for sure, there was no going back.

MY CURRENT SITUATION   BY   MARLON MCCAULSKY

Deja vs. Goliath

"Yo! What's this?" Mike bellowed and frowned, holding a piece of lingerie.

Starr had laid out some lingerie for her birthday night she planned to surprise her boyfriend, Tariq, with. She wanted to make her twenty first birthday, not just the mark of her adulthood, but the night she became a woman. But as usual, her brother was throwing a wet towel on her plans. Coming home and finding him in her bedroom was a complete disregard of her personal space.

She frowned. "What are you doing in my room?"

"No, why do you have stuff like this?"

She walked toward him and snatched it out of his hands.

"It's nightwear."

Mike scoffed. "More like ho wear. You only wear shit like this for someone else when you planning to do something."

Starr glared at him. "It's none of your business why or who I'm wearing anything for. I'm grown."

"Just because you're turning twenty-one doesn't mean you need to be out giving it up to these fools. There's nothing wrong with saving your virginity for someone you're truly in love with."

"What wait a minute?" She rubbernecked him. "I know you ain't telling me to save it when I know you and Kima been getting it in since high school!"

"That's different."

"No it's not! You're not my daddy so I would appreciate you staying out of my business!"

22

"Is that why you're having a secret birthday bash tonight without inviting me?" He made air quotes with his fingers. "Yeah, I know all about it."

"Oh my god!" She huffed. "Why are you snooping on me?"

"Because you don't know these fools out here like I do. You're smart and got a bright future ahead of you. You don't need to get caught dealing with these punk ass dudes. I'm just trying to look out for you."

She rolled her eyes. "That's not even necessary, Mike. I'm good."

She started pushing him out of her room.

"Oh really? So you plan on giving it up to that little Tariq dude."

Starr was shocked that Mike even knew his name. She had been dating Tariq for almost eight months now. They met on campus and she's only told Deja about him. She had gone out of her way to keep any information about her love life out of her brother's nosey radar.

"How do you know his name?"

Mike grinned. "It's my business to know. He plays for the Georgia Bulldogs and I know he's a ho. We used to play for the same team. He done ran up in half the freshman class at Spelman. Bet you didn't know that. You really wanna be another notch on his belt? Is that what you're doing?"

"Oh my god!" She screamed. "Get out!"

She pushed him out of her room and slammed the door.

Mike was taught since he was a child that keeping his promises were the most important thing a man can do. It's something his father instilled into him before he passed away. One of those promises he made to his father was to always look after his sister. Being a popular jock in school, Mike saw first-hand how dudes dogged girls out, especially his best friends, Jason and Rick. So when Starr's body started to fill out in junior high and boys started to notice, he decided to use his size to scare them off. He didn't care if he looked like an asshole; he was simply protecting his sister.

He had just found out his sister was dating Tariq and was disappointed that she was with a jock. Even more upset that she hadn't introduced him. Football players were notorious man whores in his days at Georgia State. He knew that nothing much had changed since was drafted into the NFL a month ago. Mike was going to begin rookie training camp in two months, plus his new wife, Kima, was now pregnant. Even with all that he had going on in his life he still made time to look after his little sister. He was annoyed when he saw the invite for her birthday party on a mutual friend's Facebook page and he wasn't invited. No doubt she didn't want him to meet Tariq, so he decided to come through and make the introduction himself. Contrary to what her brother may have thought, Starr was not the naïve little girl he thought she was. She was fully aware of Tariq's past and it wasn't a concern for her because he had been loyal since they've been together. This was her twenty first birthday and it was gonna be lit. And she'd be damn if she let her brother mess things up.

~ ~ ~

WEST END ATLANTA - DORMS

Deja moved to the dorms the first chance she got. She loved having the freedom to do what she wanted, when she wanted. She was sitting Indian style on her twin bed with a tee shirt and boy shorts on, confirming the invites for Starr's birthday party on her laptop. Lying under the covers next to her was her cut buddy, Tommy.

Tommy wasn't her man, boyfriend, main dude, side piece or any other label that implied any type of commitment. She made sure he understood that too. He was just a handsome brother who she shared an Ethics class with. In her mind, she was too young to be committed to any man before she got her life together. Her future was the most important thing to her. She just needed to get her rocks off every now and then. She heard a knock at her door and got up to answer it.

"Who is it?"

"Starr."

She opened the door and let her in.

"What's wrong with you," Deja asked, noticing the aggravated expression on her face.

"Mike," she groaned, taking a seat at the small desk by the window.

Deja snickered. "What he do now?"

"First of all, when I came home I caught his ass in my room. Had the nerve to question me about the teddy I bought the other day, touching it and shit."

"Oh, gross." Deja frowned. "Continue."

"Then he proceeds to tell me I need to remain a virgin till I'm married or whatnot. Like Kima and him haven't been fucking like rabbits since tenth grade. Hell, she was pregnant when they got married! Then he said he knows about Tariq."

"Damn," Deja laughed. "Your brother really is Inspector Gadget."

"I know! Then he tries to tell me what a whore he is and that he knows about the party tonight. How? I thought that was the whole reason we were doing invite only?"

"Well ... about that ..."

Starr glared at her. "What did you do?"

"Don't get mad but in order to fill the Gold Room I had to open it up for more than just invited guests."

"What? C'mon Deja! I don't want a bunch of randoms at my party."

"Listen, this is gonna work in our favor."

Starr folded her arms and pursed her lips. "How?"

"I got the Hip Hop funk group TRC to perform live!" Deja grinned smugly.

25

"Oh my god! That's incredible! They're like the hottest live act in the city right now! How did you pull that off?"

"That's because of me," a male voice responded. "My cousin is in the group."

Tommy had gotten out of bed and stood butt naked without a care in the world.

Starr's jaw hit the floor when she saw what he was swinging between his thighs. If Tariq was working with a one eyed monster like that she might have to reconsider the whole thing she had planned tonight.

She covered her mouth. "Oh my."

Deja frowned. "Put's some pants on fool!"

Tommy grinned, achieving his goal of showing Starr what he was packing. He didn't know she was a virgin until he overheard them talking and thought since he and Deja were only cut buddies he'd advertise his services. He found his pants on the floor and put them on.

"Why didn't you tell me Tommy was in here?" Starr asked, still in shock.

"I honestly forgot."

"Girl, you know you can't forget this," he chimed in.

She looked back at him. "Getcho nasty ass out."

"You know you like it." He smiled. "Call me later okay?"

She grinned. "Whatever, bye."

He waved to Starr on his way out and she busted out laughing as soon as he closed the door.

"Got damn, Deja! I know you said he was a monster but damn! How do you even handle all of … that."

"Well, they don't call me Wonder Woman for nothing." She shrugged. "Anyway; like he said, I got his cousin to get the band to perform and paid them a modest fee. Our invited guests get in for free and everybody else pays twenty-five at the door. I cut a deal with the club and we get thirty percent of the profit on the backend!"

Starr jumped up and hugged her friend. "That's so dope! We should go into business doing this!"

"The thought crossed my mind." She laughed. "Don't worry about Mike. He's just being his regular annoying self. You just make sure you ready for Tariq. You've had that brother waiting faithfully for months. He gonna loose his mind when he gets his hands on you."

Starr bit her bottom lip. "Oh I hope so, because I'm so ready."

~~~

BUCKHEAD ATLANTA - THE GOLD ROOM

Just as Deja planned, Starr's birthday was a huge success. The club was packed with people who mostly paid to see TRC perform live. The thirty percent kickback they would get was good business. They both saw the potential in doing something like this on a more professional level in the future. That was a conversation they would both have soon; but as for the night, there was nothing more on Starr's mind than partying and being with Tariq.

Tariq Gibson was a star running back for the Bulldogs and was having a record setting season. At six foot two, Tariq was a handsome chocolate brother with Lance Gross like features. He was the type of brother Starr loved. Being the curvy size beauty she was Tariq quickly took notice after seeing her at a Frat party the Kappa's were throwing one fall night. Starr wasn't a groupie and didn't throw herself at him like so many other girls typically did. That intrigued him and made him pursue her unlike any girl he had before. And after a few dates of seeing what a good girl she was made him want her even more. She made Tariq prove that he wasn't just trying to hit and run. Soon after, they started going steady for months and as tempted as she was to give herself to him she decided to make him wait.

Tonight, Starr was not holding anything back as she danced and grinded on him. She didn't give a damn what her brother thought about him she was grown enough to make

27

her own decisions. They partied in the VIP section on the second level of the Gold Room with Deja and were surrounded by most of her friends she invited. The upper level had a great view of the dance floor of the club as the party was jumping. TRC was on stage rocking the house.

Deja was happy knowing that her bestie was going to finally get her cherry popped and it wasn't gonna be by no scrub. She admired that she held on to her virginity as long as she had. Lord knows if she had a chance to go back she wouldn't have given it up to the guy she did, but that was water under the bridge now. Deja looked at her friend enjoying herself and was happy for her but as she gazed out into the crowd she spotted him. She couldn't believe it. Mike had shown up. It was easy to spot him. He was the only one not dancing, but weaving through the crowed obviously searching for his sister. Deja watched intensely. There was no way she was gonna let him ruin this night.

As Mike made his way through the sea of party goers he unexpectedly came face-to-face with a familiar petite surprise.

"What are you doing here, Mike?" Deja quizzed in sharp tone.

"Hey Deja, just came through to wish my sister a happy birthday. Where is she?"

"This is sad. Why do you do this? Starr is twenty-one years old now. It's been past time for you to stop acting like she's a child!"

Mike rolled his eyes. "Listen Deja, I know she's your best friend but I'm her brother. Just because you and Dani aren't close, I am with my sister."

Deja frowned. She didn't like that he brought up her relationship with Danielle as if that had anything to do with why he was there.

"You're so full shit, Mike. You're just here to harass Tariq. You have a pregnant wife at home and you're here messing with your sister? Grow up!"

Mike glanced up toward the VIP section. "She's up there isn't she?" He tried to step by Deja but she blocked his path. "Move Deja."

"No. Go home, Mike."

It was like David facing off against Goliath without all the biblical importance. Deja may have been a small woman but she was as fierce as a lioness when it came to her friend.

Mike shook his head and exhaled. "Deja, you are literally five-foot-three and ninety-five pounds soaking wet. I can pick you up with one hand and move you out my way."

"I dare you," she challenged.

They locked eyes in a standoff. His hulking frame towered over her tiny body. Deja called his bluff and he knew it but she wasn't backing down.

"For crying out loud Deja, she's my sister. I just wanna see her."

She folded her arms. "And you will—tomorrow. Bye Mike."

He glanced up toward the VIP section and saw his little sister hugging Tariq, then looked back at Deja in front of him. As annoyed as he was, he respected Deja for standing her ground. This was a battle he wasn't going to win tonight. He would meet up with Tariq soon enough. He shook his head in defeat, turned around, and head toward the exit. Deja snickered, she thought Mike was crazy but respected his protectiveness. She kind of wished she and Danielle had that closeness but there was too much resentment between them for that to happen. She turned and went back up to the VIP once she made sure Mike was gone.

For the rest of the night Starr enjoyed the party and later, in a suite at the Hyatt Atlanta Midtown, Tariq enjoyed her. She was nervous; but to his credit, Tariq was a gentleman and took his time with her. He admired her thickness in the lace black teddy she bought. Her body was a black man's fantasy come true. When she finally saw what he was working with her mind flashed back to the sight of Tommy in Deja's dorm room. She was astonished that Tariq appeared to be more endowed than him. The little bit of pain she felt at first was soon replaced by overwhelming pleasure as they found a groove and made love. In her mind, this was the best birthday gift she could have ever received.

Expensive Taste

The annual V-103 Car and Bike show was in full swing by the time Jason arrived. Over thirty-thousand people flock to this showcase to look at the custom cars and motorcycles but he was there to admire something else even more exotic—women. The vehicles may have been on display but the beautiful women in Atlanta were the real draw, for him at least. Thick or slim, short or tall, light or dark, he loved them all.

Today, he was rolling solo. Normally Rick would have been his wingman but he moved to LA for a job with the Lakers a few months ago. After the fiasco at his mother's house and break-up with Dani, Rick had little reason to stay in Atlanta. So after Mike and Kima got married he moved out west.

As Jason was walking through the venue he noticed a couple of ladies that he had random hook ups with. He was either greeted with sexy smiles or raised middle fingers, depending on their last interaction. He was amused by both; but today, he was interested in exploring new territory. Being the seasoned hunter he was, Jason could quickly spot the sandpits in the crowd. Women with fake butts, horse weave down to their ass, or a tribe of kids following them around the show were easy to spot. And in this mob there were a lot of them. A lot of other attractive women already had men marking their territory and mean mugging anybody looking too hard at their trophies.

As he was navigating his way through the crowd he saw her looking like a queen amongst little girls. It was only a glimpse at first before she vanished in the crowd but Jason tracked his prey and got his eyes back on the target within seconds. She was gorgeous. She had a pixie haircut that showed off her sexy neckline, high cheekbones, and caramel complexion. High end fashion clothes on a body meant for high end modeling in Paris. She looked to be with another female who had similar features and he wondered if they were related. He followed them, admiring the way she moved and caught a glimpse of her smile. She was enjoying herself. Her friend spotted him and brought his attention to her. She glanced back and saw him admiring her. Jason wasn't shy about his voyeurism. Their eyes met and the attraction was mutual. She made note of his presence with a smile but moved on. He continued to follow her through the crowd until he saw her making her way toward the exit. He moved quickly and caught up with her.

"Leaving so soon?"

She smiled. "Is there a reason I should stay?"

Her accent caught his attention. It wasn't from Atlanta or anywhere down south, it was somewhere up north. She wasn't local. He liked it and stepped closer.

"Yeah, I think it would be a shame if you didn't get a chance to know me."

She folded her arms. "Really? I thought you were just going to follow us the whole time."

Her friend chuckled.

"Just giving you and your friend space to take in the atmosphere." He glanced at her, smiled and nodded. "But yeah, my name is Jason."

He extended his hand toward her. She looked and then shook it. "Selena."

"Rashida," her friend chimed in. He shook her hand as well. She was very attractive; dressed in a colorful short flowing Dashiki dress. Her long dreadlocs hung loosely down her back complementing her attractive face. She looked like she could have been from any of the Caribbean Islands or Africa itself. Jason would've tried to talk to her but there was something about Selena that held his attention. Rashida took no offense from his obvious attraction to her friend. Besides, she was already happily in a relationship.

"Nice to meet you both. So how long have you been in Atlanta?"

"What makes you think I ain't from the A?"

"That right there." He smirked. "You just tried too hard to force that colloquialism out. That ain't you baby girl. You ain't a native. New Yorker?"

Selena smiled. "Manhattan."

"I'm from here," Rashida said.

He nodded. "Oh I know, I saw you doing the Bankhead bounce a few minutes ago, so…"

They all laughed.

"And where are you from?" Selena quizzed.

"Born in Savannah, raised in Decatur where it's greater."

"You sure about that? You don't seem like some of these other southern boys I've run into around here."

"See that's where you're making your mistake. There ain't nobody around here like me. I'm a unique experience unlike any man you've ever had before."

"That was good!" Selena laughed. "I see what you did there."

"You did? I was wondering if it was too soon to go for the double entendre. You set me up for it so I had to take it."

She smiled. "I would have been disappointed if you didn't."

They laughed some more. Each of them sizing the other up. Both liking what they were seeing.

"But really, can I call you some time or what?"

She gazed at him. "How about you join me at a private get together tonight I'm having at the W?"

He nodded. "Sounds good to me."

Rashida smiled at the obvious chemistry between the two. She was hoping that her friend would meet someone to snap her out of the funk she had been in lately. Selena had recently moved back to Atlanta from New York after a bad break up and reconnected with her college friend. Rashida encouraged her to come out with her to the Car and Bike show. Reluctantly she agreed but after meeting Jason she was glad she took her friend's advice. They exchanged information and parted ways shortly afterward. Just by their brief conversation Jason could tell by the way she talked and how she carried herself Selena was educated and financially well off. The invite to a private event at the W verified that much. He wasn't intimated by her status at all. In Jason's mind even an upper class chick was a freak in the dark too.

THE W HOTEL ATLANTA - MIDTOWN

Later that night Jason went to the W Hotel in midtown Atlanta. After checking in at the desk, he received the passcode for rooftop access and he rode the elevator to the top. He stepped off the lift and walked to the pool bar. It was perfect place to party on a hot summer night. It was an intimate gathering, scantily dressed women and men wearing swimming trunks and Gucci flip flops were enjoying themselves. Neo-soul R&B was playing. Jason felt overdressed for the occasion wearing black jeans and a short sleeved gray button down. As he walked toward the poolside he saw Selena wearing a baby blue lace up dress that stopped mid-thigh. He was aroused by her, and of course, was ready to divide and conquer what was between her thighs. He walked toward her and she smiled seeing him again.

"Glad you could make it!" She greeted him with a hug and a sweet vanilla scent filled his nostrils. The way she felt next to his body stimulated all his senses and made him want to hold onto her longer. He fought the temptation and slowly let go.

"I'm glad you invited me. Nice view."

"Yeah, the city is beautiful at night."

He affixed his eyes on her. "That's not the only thing

that looks good at night."

She smiled.

"Where's your friend, Rashida?" He asked.

"She's kicking it with her man. Nice of you to ask about her."

"Well I've been told that I'm a very thoughtful kind of guy."

She smirked. "Hmmm … I bet you are." She gestured to the lawn chairs next to the pool and they had a seat. Immediately, a server came by and offered him a glass of champagne. He slipped it and sat back.

Selena watched him. "You seem to be very comfortable."

"Why wouldn't I be?"

"Most guys I invite to something like this kinda get intimidated."

He smiled. "I told you, I'm not like most guys."

She sipped her drink. "So tell me about yourself. What made you move to Atlanta from Savannah?"

"Well, I moved here when I was five. My Dad relocated us after he and my Mom divorced."

"Oh, so did you go back and forth to be with your mother?"

"Nah." Jason groaned slightly. "My Mom had issues. Drug abuse. So I didn't see much of her growing up. I mean she's good now but we're not that close. I'm actually a lot closer to my best friend's Mom than my own."

"I see. I guess we have more in common than I thought. I was mostly raised by my father and whatever nanny was on his payroll at the time."

"You're not close with your Mom?"

"Not by choice. She passed away when I was little."

"Sorry."

"No worries. It was a long time ago."

"So you're a Daddy's girl huh?"

"Not quite. I think he wanted a boy but got stuck

with me. We have a complicated relationship. He doesn't approve of my life choices."

Jason nodded with understanding. "So I guess we're both who we are because of our parents."

"Now that's scary." She shook her head and slightly huffed. "I've literally just met you and I'm talking about my daddy issues; but for some reason, I feel comfortable talking to you."

He took another sip of his drink. "Yeah, I feel the same way too. So what did you do that your father disapproves of?"

Jason noticed the change in her body language. "He's a very successful real estate tycoon. Not my thing. I've been modeling since I was fourteen but I want to get into fashion. Designing my own clothing line. That type of thing."

"I can see that happening for you. So you're a model." He nodded. "Makes sense."

"What makes you think that?"

"The way you move, the way you dress, I can tell."

She smirked. "So, you like models?"

"Who doesn't?" He questioned enthusiastically. "And for the record you're the first real model I've ever dated. Instagram doesn't count."

"Dating? Is that what we're doing now?"

"Of course. I've already made it through the first contact phase. You know where you asked yourself, if you were attracted to me. That's why I got the invite. Check. So this is the getting to know you phase. Making sure you ain't crazy and deranged. If we have anything in common. Check."

Oh," she snickered, "so you got this all figured out?"

"I'm familiar with the process." Jason showcased his million dollar smile.

"Hmmm … so what's the sex phase?"

"Now, that can vary," he admitted. "Some woman do the three date rule so they ain't thought of as a ho. Some women just wanna bone so they're down for a one night stand and then ghost on ya. But I think all women make up their mind as soon as they meet a man, if they're going to sleep with him or not."

She leaned in closer. "So do you know what I've decided?"

He studied her. "I got a theory."

Selena leaned back in her chair and sipped her drink. Jason noticed her sly smile and did the same. To his surprise they spent the rest of the night getting to know each other while drinking expensive drinks. It was the first time he met a woman who could match his wit and keep him on his toes. It was four o'clock in the morning when they found themselves alone on the rooftop. As much as he wanted to sleep with her, Jason was surprised he was enjoying himself simply talking to her. Being around her felt good. He glanced at his watch and decided to call it a night. She walked with him to the elevator then wrapped her arms around his neck. The city lights sparkled in the darkness making the atmosphere on the rooftop feel even more romantic.

"Jason, you are so different than I thought you were."

"Really? How so?"

"I know you're not into relationships. I know you're into getting it in with as many women as you humanly can. I get it. You're young, smart, handsome, and don't want a commitment."

"So why did you invite me here tonight?" He locked eyes with her.

"I was curious." She gave him a once over from head to toe then she kissed him.

They kissed each other slowly and passionately. Jason felt his manhood rise. He wanted her in every way possible. Their lips broke apart and he spoke in hushed tones.

"So, was I right in my theory?"

"Yes, you were. I'm going to sleep with you, just not tonight."

He nodded. "You playing hard to get?"

"When I decide to sleep with you, you'll know it," She kissed him again.

~~~

It wasn't until weeks later that they actually had sex and somewhere in the mix Jason fell head over heels in love with this woman and she for him. She was the first woman he ever admitted that to. This was the first time he ever let a woman in this deep. All the things he criticized Rick for doing for Danielle he was now doing for Selena. He was happily breaking every playa rule he knew for her. With the type of money Selena had they took trips to St. Bart's and the Bahamas frequently. They danced in the raunchiest clubs and made passionate love all night on the beach. They were living a hedonistic lifestyle for two months, engaged in the pursuit of pleasure.

He only told Rick about her and he couldn't believe it. Even Jason had a hard time believing what he was feeling. Love was for suckers, not him, but here was looking like a sucker and not giving a damn. For the first time in his life he could see a future with a woman. His feelings had grown to the point where he wanted to be more than just lovers. One day he showed up at her suite and knocked on her door. He waited but no one answered. Rang the bell and no one came. He pulled out his cell, dialed her number then heard a message saying it had been disconnected. He went down to the front desk. He had been coming to the W to see her so often that he was on a first name basis with the employees.

"Hey Jennifer, have you seen Selena today?"

She had an uneasy look on her face. "I'm sorry Mr. Trammell but she checked out early this morning."

"What do you mean checked out? I was just here with her yesterday."

Solemnly, Jennifer handed him an envelope with his name written on it. He took it and opened it.

Dear Jason, my love. These past few months with you have been the best of my life. I've never been with anyone like you. For reasons I can't explain, I have to go. I wish that I had the courage to say it to your face but I know if I saw you I could never leave. Please don't try to find me. I'm so sorry but I have no choice. Loving you always. Selena XOXO"

Jason's heart broke reading her words. What could have happened to make her leave him like this? Why couldn't she tell him? Questions he didn't have an answer for frustrated him but more so angered him. There was no forwarding address. The only woman he ever loved was gone without reason and he felt like a fool. The only other woman who ever hurt him so deeply was his birth mother when he was a child but this pain was different—more profound. This made him feel hollow inside. He promised himself that he would never let another woman hurt him like this again. He was done with love.

SIX YEARS LATER

DejaStarr

ATLANTA - DEJASTARR ENTERTAINMENT, LLC

"Okay boys, it's time to get naked!"

Deja stood in their conference room in front five half naked men with a big grin on her face. Deja and Starr were business partners in DejaStarr Entertainment. A company they founded soon after college and built from the ground up over the last four years; even though Deja didn't finish her last year of school. They were the best at party planning, online promotions, graphic and web design.

Every one of the well-toned bodies stood in front of them glistened with baby oil. Her fingers glided over cell phone and the raunchy melodies of Jodeci played through the surround sound.

Both women were all smiles as they watched the men shake, jiggle, and gyrate. Slowly, each dancer pulled down their shorts and revealed why they were known as the Dickem' Down Boys. Personally, neither Deja nor Starr would ever mess with any of the Double D Boys for a number of reasons. The number one reason was there was no telling how many women they have dicked down over their stellar two year career. But that didn't mean they weren't a pleasure to watch.

Starr raised a curious eyebrow. "They are certainly are talented."

"Gifted."

"Blessed."

"Hung like fucking horses," Deja whispered. They both laughed and continued to watch the private show.

As they wound their way around the men and danced along with them, their play time was cut short.

"What in the world!"

Quickly, their heads turned toward the door. They

weren't expecting any guests, let alone, Danielle. Her mouth fell open seeing the sights before her.

Starr quickly stopped the music. Deja glanced at her sister and let a shit eating grin cover her face. Then she turned her attention to the men.

"Gentlemen, I think this audition went quite well. We'll be in touch with you all very soon. You can get dressed in the back."

Starr walked over to Danielle. "Hey, how are you?"

"In a state of disbelief." She watched the men disappear from the room.

She gave her a nervous smile. "It wasn't what it looked like. We're throwing a bachelorette party at the Opera House in two weeks."

She looked at Deja who obviously enjoyed her shock. "Oh, I see."

"Well, I'm gonna make sure our … um … guests get shown to the door." Starr grinned. "I'll talk to you later, Dani."

"Later."

She exited the room.

"I wasn't expecting you to come by," Deja admitted, and had a seat at the conference table.

"Apparently. I see you were in the middle of doing … work."

Deja blushed. "I can't help it if my job is more fun than yours."

"Whatever." Danielle sat down. "I came by to see if you made the arrangements for dad's birthday party."

Deja rolled her eyes. "And like I told you before—"

Before she could finish, Deja's cell vibrated. She glanced at the caller ID, sent it to voicemail and finished. "I got this."

"Then please share the details with me." She crossed her arms and waited.

"Dani," Deja sighed, "whether you believe it or not, I

have work to do so I don't have time to explain every little detail to you. I do this for a living. I do it in my sleep too." Deja gyrated in her seat just to irritate her sister.

Danielle narrowed her eyes at her sister. "I know you do but this isn't a bachelor party for some horny frat boys. This is our father."

"Well damn, let's go 'head and cancel the Twerk Team and send back the Budweiser keg I ordered! Once again, Dani, you stopped me from making a mess of things. I appreciate it. Let me see if I can get a hold of Shirley Ceasar. Dad will really like that."

Danielle glared at her sister for a second, not amused at her over the top sarcasm. Why couldn't she understand how important this was to her? Why couldn't she just take this a bit more serious?

Deja returned her sister's frown hoping that she got the message that she didn't care what she thought, she was going to do it her way. Period.

Danielle exhaled.

Message received.

Danielle got up from the table. "Fine. Just give me a heads up on what the plan is."

"If I need your help, I'll let you know."

She nodded, made her way to the door and left. Deja sat for a minute pissed at her sister's lack of faith in her. She already had the plans set for their father. A nice dinner at his favorite Jamaican restaurant followed by some good live reggae at Legends Café in the VIP section with his friends. She could've explained it all to her in two minutes but she didn't feel the need to. She wasn't her mother. Deja shook her head, reached for her phone, and dialed the number back that called a few minutes ago.

A mischievous smile came across her face when she heard his voice. "I had company. Wus up?"

She paused momentarily, then responded, "Yeah it was Dani. I wouldn't have called you back if she was still here."

She listened to his seductive tone then replied, "Yeah that sounds good."

"Why don't you come through about eleven?" She licked her lips. "Yeah, I'll still be up. Later."

She ended the call, thought about what he said, anticipating what the night would bring.

This Is A Stick Up

LOS ANGELES, CA

"Yes! Don't stop!" She moaned as he gave her another deep stroke from behind. Rick loved being a bachelor. LA had an assortment of attractive women that seemed to be impossible to avoid. Tonight he found himself in the bed of yet another gorgeous woman. She thought this was probably some of the best sex she had in years. After being so sexually frustrated for so long she felt like she needed this fuck more than air itself.

"Yeah baby ... just... like ... that.... Aaahhh!" Rick felt the walls of her vagina tightening around his penis. He knew this must had been fate for them to have met the way they did. There she was sitting courtside at the Lakers game checking him out as if he was one of the starting five instead of being one of the team trainers. Her brown sugar complexion caught his eye. The Lakers crop top she wore exposed her sexy abs. The swell of her breasts made her tee struggle to hold them back and the way her fat ass looked in the black skin tight leggings she wore was obscene. That was more than enough reason for him to introduce himself.

After a few drinks, some dirty dancing, and small talk at a nearby bar, Carla invited Rick back to her place. There was no need to waste time. As soon as the front door closed, Carla was on him, and Rick had no problem accommodating her desire. He found it ironic that when he woke up this morning, he was a single man between relationships and by nightfall he was in single woman's bed deep between her legs. He withdrew from her wetness and she rolled on her back.

She grinned. "You're amazing."

"I'm just getting started, baby." Rick slid his length back inside of her.

Carla gasped feeling his long hard member moving in

and out of her again. "I hope … aahh … I hope you… ah … don't think I do this all the time."

Rick stared in her eyes and continued to stroke her. "Do what?"

"Take guys home I just met. I'm not a whore." She bit her bottom lip as he slid in deep, hit bottom, and held that position for a few seconds. "You just turn me on so much."

"Just lay back and relax." He smiled. "Let me do all the work."

He kissed her lips and continued to work her slowly. Carla dug her nails into his back as she moved her hips back and forth matching the tempo. She felt good knowing that he didn't think any less of her for inviting him in her bed after only knowing him for a few hours. It had been so long since she had some good dick that she felt like she deserved to be a freak for one night.

Meeting a man as fine as Rick was the perfect excuse she needed to cut loose. Seeing his sexy chocolate ass next to the players, but in a suit, got her panties wet. He was just her type—the type who could get it any way and anywhere he wanted.

It wasn't long before Carla found herself having one of the best orgasms she ever had in her life. Rick could tell by her moans and convulsions that he had put in some good work. Now that she got hers he went extra hard to get his. If there was one thing he had mastered over the years was how to please a woman. He knew if a woman was not satisfied sexually the word would spread to other women like wildfire. He had seen it done to countless other men and he promised to never be one.

In the midst of their tryst, Carla heard a sound that brought fear into her heart like she had never felt before. She paused and her eyes became wide like saucers. Rick noticed how tense she had become.

"What's wrong, baby?"

"Oh my god … did you hear that?"

"Hear what?" He looked around, confused.

"My garage door just opened!"

"You sure? Somebody's breaking in your house?"

She reached over and turned on her lamp. "No! My husband came back in town early!"

"Your husband? You're married?"

Rick glanced around her bedroom and to his surprise, he saw quite a few pictures of Carla and her husband. It was dark when he was invited into her bedroom so he never noticed.

He jumped off of her and quickly found his boxers. "Why didn't you tell you were married?"

Carla got up and put on her robe. "You didn't ask."

Rick stared at her in shock. "I didn't ask? I shouldn't have to ask! That's vital information that's usually volunteered when I meet a woman for the first time!"

Carla looked at him as she pulled the sheets off the bed. "I thought you knew."

Rick quickly grab the condom he was using and shoved it in his pocket. "How the hell was I supposed to know that? You don't even have on a ring!"

"Oh thanks for reminding me." She went into her dresser drawer, pulled out her ring and slid it on her finger.

"Oh now yo ass wanna put it on!"

"I never had a one night stand before so if I told you I was married you wouldn't have had sex with me!"

Rick stared at her body for a second. He knew he wouldn't have passed on that ass either way. "That's not the point! You shoulda told me! I wouldn't have come back to your house had I known!"

"That doesn't matter, you gotta go! If my husband finds you up in here he'll kill both of us!"

"No really! Where am I supposed to go? We're on the second floor!"

"You gotta hide! The closet!"

He frowned. "That's the first place he'll look! Hey

does he have a gun?"

"James? No."

Rick quickly put on his pants and shirt. Then they both heard the door downstairs close. He felt his heart race not believing he was in this situation. He knew that a man would kill another man if he found him with his wife.

Rick looked at Carla. "You gotta stall him before he comes up!"

"How?"

"Girl, you better think of something!"

A panicked expression painted her face. Then she exhaled, went to the bedroom door and cracked it open. "James is that you?" She called out.

"Yeah babe!" They heard a male voice reply. "I decided to leave the convention early."

Rick shook his head in total disbelief this shit was happening to him for real.

"Oh okay, babe can you bring something to drink before you come up? Some water?"

"Sure!"

They both exhaled knowing they bought themselves a few more seconds to think. Rick looked around her bedroom and spotted a red handkerchief on the nightstand. He had an idea.

James Hudson had been married to Carla Jones for two years after only dating for three months. For the last year he had been feeling some type of way about the marriage. The honeymoon had long been over between them.

Carla came from a rich family. She was young, naïve in relationships, and sheltered by her father. That led to her wanting to be free and sent her running to James. He saw a young woman he could mold into his ideal wife and also finance his struggling small business. At the time it just made sense to him to lock this young thing down. Caught up in what she thought was good sex, she mistook that as love, and was taken in.

Little did James know that his plan would backfire. He didn't foresee her father cutting her off financially. After burning through her little savings on more bad business decisions he found himself back in the same position he started in. Carla; however, got tired of being a kept woman and realized that her single girlfriends were living it up. She became restless. Plus hearing her friend's stories about the crazy orgasmic sex they were having on the regular, she realized her experiences with James were nowhere close. Sex between them soon became a chore more than it was for pleasure.

James found himself going on business trips to make money. Even more trips once he met a professional independent freak out on the Vegas strip one night. The last thing he was thinking that Carla was getting her freak on too. There was nothing holy about this matrimony.

James grabbed a bottle of water from the fridge and made his way upstairs. He opened his bedroom door and saw Carla sitting on the bed.

"Hey baby, you miss me?"

She gave him a nervous smile. "I've been counting every minute you've been gone."

"Good, cause I been counting all the different ways I'm gonna tear yo ass up." He walked toward her.

Rick's heart raced knowing he was in a real life or death situation and exhaled quietly. Like it or not he knew what he had to do. James closed the door and Rick crept up on him from behind.

"This is a stick up!" He threatened through clinched teeth.

James felt a hard object in his ribcage and panic filled his heart.

"Oh shit, oh god!"

"Shut the fuck up fool!" Rick bellowed.

Rick, by no stretch of the imagination, was a thug. Nor had he ever committed a crime. He graduated summa cum laude from Clark Atlanta University but tonight he was gonna apply all his years of watching Boyz In Da Hood, Juice, Belly and all of the other gangsta flicks he ever watched into this moment.

"Please don't kill me, please don't me kill me, you can take anything you want," James pleaded. "PLEASE! Oh god ... don't hurt me!"

Rick was taken off guard at how submissive James had become. He was expecting a little more confidence. Suddenly, everybody smelled a distinctive odor in the air.

"What the ..." He sniffed. "Did you just pee on yourself?"

Tears rimmed James' eyes. "Sorry."

Carla was embarrassed by her husband's lack of courage in this situation. Granted, she knew that this scenario was bogus and that Rick had the wooden handle of her hairbrush in James's ribcage but what if this was a real home invasion? Is this how her husband, the man who's supposed to protect her at all costs, would react? Rick caught the look of shame on Carla's face and knew he had to end this situation before anything else awkward occurred. James was shaking like a leaf.

"Man, just give me your money."

James quickly went in his pocket and pulled out his wallet. He was fumbling so much that as he was opening his wallet a Trojan condom fell out and hit the floor in front of Carla.

Rick sighed, knowing that this fool had just made this situation even more disastrous for himself.

"Oh shit," James whispered.

Carla's eyes widened and then her face contorted into a scowl. "Is that a fucking condom?"

"Baby, it's ... it's not what it looks like," James stammered.

With the speed and agility that defied description, Carla pounced on James like a black panther. She punched and slapped him mercilessly. Rick was completely taken off guard by her attack on her husband.

"You asshole! You've been fucking some ho in Vegas! Is that why you've been taking all these *business* trips every month!?"

"Baby please! I … I … can explain," James pleaded covering his face from her violent assault.

Rick quickly backed off not wanting to get caught in her war path. He hastily took the opportunity to run out of the room and get the hell out of their house. Even after he got outside he could still hear Carla ripping her husband a new one. He couldn't help but think to himself how ironic it was that she was just screwing him but she's going crazy finding out her husband was cheating too. He shook his head, got in his car parked across the street and pulled off.

As Rick drove back to his apartment he glanced at his phone and saw that he had missed a call and a voicemail. He listened to the message.

"Hello Mr. Westbrook, this is Dr. Lefkovits from Northside Hospital, your mother's physician. I need to give you some very important information regarding the current state of her health. If you can please call the hospital as soon as possible at this number…"

MY CURRENT SITUATION   BY   MARLON MCCAULSKY

My Sisters Keeper

UNION CITY - MIKE & KIMA'S HOUSE

"Trust me, dad, we have everything planned out for you," Danielle assured, but mainly trying to convince herself as she spoke over Bluetooth of her newly purchased Benz. She was on her way to Mike and Kima's house when she got a phone call from her father, Winston Queen.

Mike and Kima lived in a modest 4 bedroom brick home in an upscale subdivision in Union City. Mike spent five years in the NFL playing for the Atlanta Falcons before a knee injury forced him to retire. Fortunately, Mike had Kima invested his money and because of her visions, they owned three sports memorabilia stores across Atlanta. Kima was now a stay at home wife raising their girls and she loved it.

This was the kind of neighborhood that was perfect to raise kids in. The kind of place Danielle could have seen herself living if things would have turned out as she planned.

"Really? So you and Deja are really working together?"

"Yeah."

"You mean Deja ... your sister right?"

"Of course dad," she responded dryly. "Who else would I be talking about?"

"I'm just saying. You two don't have the best track record when it comes to getting along."

Danielle couldn't deny that. The term oil and water was them in a nutshell. She's never worked well with Deja. In the past they always just agreed to stay out of each other's way and if things came together in the end, it was just a happy accident.

"Well trust me, dad, I'm going to make sure you have the best birthday night ever." She pulled into Kima's driveway and parked.

"That's good hear, baby girl. Just call me later, okay?"

"Okay dad. Talk to you later."

"Alright, bye." He ended the call.

Danielle sat in her car wondering if she could really make good on her promise to make her father's birthday night all that. After all, his 60th had to be special. Danielle wanted to give Deja the benefit of the doubt especially since she chose event planning as a career choice, but her flashback to the mostly naked men concerned her. Could Deja really be trusted to pull together something classy? She already had a backup plan though, just in case.

Danielle got out of her car and walked to the front door. Just as she was going to knock the door flew open and standing there was her five year old goddaughter, Kennedy.

With a wide smile she yelled, "Hi auntie, Dani!"

"Well, hello to you too, sunshine!"

She bent down and gave her a huge hug.

"You're such a big girl now!" Danielle lifted her off her feet.

Danielle carried Kennedy on her hip, went inside the house and closed the door with her free hand. She adored her as if she were her own. She always talked to her when Kima was pregnant and was there when she was born. Kima made Danielle Kennedy's godmother, a role she took very seriously so Kennedy literally had two mothers looking after her. And when they had their second daughter, Kimberly, she was there for her too.

As Danielle walked through the foyer into the living room she could smell the incredible meal Kima was in the kitchen cooking. If there was one thing Danielle wished she could do, was to be able to cook like her. *She must have been born with a spatula in her hand*, she thought. Kima saw Danielle shuffle into the kitchen with Kennedy and smiled.

"You know she is too big for you to be carrying around like that."

"What, this is my baby!" Danielle gave Kennedy a kiss

on the cheek.

"Really? You know I can go pack a bag for her right now." She covered the pot she was checking. "Let you keep her for the next, ummm, thirteen years or so."

"Why would I do that when I can leave her here with you and just visit?" She put Kennedy down. "Go play little mama."

Kennedy ran out of the kitchen and back upstairs to her room.

"You better stop offering people your kids."

Kima grinned. "Not people, just you."

"I'ma tell Mike. Where is he?"

"He's in the backyard playing with that old rusty grill."

Danielle sat on a stool at the kitchen island. "He's planning on barbequing a lot this summer huh?"

"As usual, he starts thinking he's Bobby Flay when he's on that thing. *This was my daddy's grill and his father's grill before that. And I'ma pass it down to our son'*, she imitated her husband's voice.

She smiled. "Let him have his fun. Wait a minute? You have girls … what son is he talking about? You knocked up again?"

"No!" Kima shot back. "But if that mad man out there has anything to say about I will be. He's trying his best to put another one up in me."

"He wants a boy."

Kima sat at the island with her. "Yeah well, there's nothing I can do about that."

Danielle looked around the house. "Where's that cat of yours?"

She sighed. "I think Snuffles went out the backyard and got lost."

"Good, that damn cat was evil."

"Snuffles is not evil. Why would you say that?"

"Oh c'mon Kima, that cat was the spawn of Satan,

always hissing and scratching at people. He gave me the creeps."

"He loved me! Anyway what's up with you?"

"I just left DejaStarr and got an eyeful of ding-a-ling swinging around the office." Danielle shook her head.

"What?"

"Apparently they're throwing some kind of bachelorette party soon. They had a group of naked greased up men in there."

"Oh, ah, any chance of them still being there?"

"Girl, your husband is out there!"

"And, what's your point? I didn't say I wanted to fuck them but hey if there are raw dicks being slung around I wouldn't mind taking a look."

"I swear you're almost as bad as Deja."

"Shit, I could use some adult entertainment in my life because if I have to listen to Baby Shark one more damn time." Kima rolled her eyes. "Anyway, stop giving your sister a hard time. Deja and Starr are doing good for themselves."

"I guess. I just wish she would take our dad's birthday celebration a little more serious."

"What makes you think she's not?"

Danielle exhaled. "When I asked her to tell me what she had planned for him she blew me off and acted like she didn't have time to tell me shit. I just wanna know if he's going to enjoy himself."

Kima gave Danielle a knowing smile. "Dani, you know how your sister is. She probably was annoyed you showed up at her place ready to cross examine her. You know how you do."

She frowned. "I don't do that!"

Kima just stared at her without saying anything. Danielle glared back knowing that she does.

"So what if I do! She's the one who insisted on handling everything. She didn't want to include me, so is it wrong for me wanting to know something? Damn!"

"Dani, despite your differences with her, you know Deja loves her father. I have no doubt she has a wonderful time planned for him. You just need to relax and let her do her thing."

"I suppose ... but she coulda told me though."

Kima got up from the island. "Anyway, are you staying for dinner?"

She looked at her with a twisted expression. "As if you had to ask."

~~~

Danielle enjoyed dinner with Kima's family but soon it was time for her to go home. As she was on the highway the Bluetooth in her car started to ring. She looked at the display and saw Northside Hospital. She pressed accept on the console.

"Hello?"

"Hello, is this Ms. Queen?" A female voice asked.

"Yes," Danielle responded, alarmed.

"Hi, this is Dr. Lefkovits. I'm Sharon Westbrook's physician. She had you listed as an emergency contact."

"Okay, what's going on?"

"Ms. Westbrook was brought into our ER this evening complaining of chest pains."

"Oh my God... is she okay?"

"I'm afraid she had a heart attack. She's in stable condition now but if you can come to Northside Hospital ..."

"Of course, I'm on my way now!"

3 Simple Rules

With her face buried in her plush white pillow and ass in the air Deja was in enjoying a mid-morning stroking from her homeboy Jason. Deja had always thought of Jason as a bit of jerk, but when it came to sex, he was a winner in her book.

She was thick in all the right places and Jason loved hitting it from the back. He loved the way her ass jiggled and Deja loved the way he felt sliding deep inside her. He gripped her hips firmly and stroked her wetness with short hard thrusts making her headboard bang against the wall. Deja muffled her screams of pleasure into her pillow as Jason manhandled her ass like savage.

Even though they've known each other for years their first time hooking up was a couple of months ago after she hosted a grand re-opening of his night club. He hired DejaStarr Entertainment because he knew they did good work. He didn't think he would end up between Deja's legs; especially considering the bad blood between him and Danielle, but after a few drinks and some dirty dancing they both felt a sexual chemistry that was undeniable. After that first night, Deja knew she wanted to see him again. She just didn't want Danielle to find out or she would never hear the end of it. Plus, she knew Jason was a man whore and being seen as a couple would make her look like a fool. Jason may not have been the man she wanted to be in a relationship with but he certainly had the credentials she needed in the bedroom.

She had a few simple rules; they only hook up when she was in the mood. Under no circumstances was he supposed to come over before calling; and last but the most important, nobody catches feelings.

"You like that, girl," Jason grunted, giving Deja

60

another deep thrust from the back.

"Aaaahhhh … yes shit … don't stop!"

She felt another hard thrust and moaned.

Jason proceeded to stroke her just the way she liked. He was in heaven feeling her wetness all around him and bit his bottom lip delivering another hard thrust. Deja was always sexy to him and for years, he always imagined how good the sex would be but had no idea it would be this good. In the midst of their freak session, Deja's cell begun to vibrate. She attempted to reach for it on her nightstand. Jason; however, was not going to be interrupted when he was so close to busting a good nut.

"Don'tcha touch that fuckin' phone!" He put more of his body weight on her and rapidly pumped inside of her.

Deja moaned with pleasure submitting to his demands allowing the incoming call to go to voicemail. For the next ten minutes Jason had his way with Deja until he finally came inside his condom. He grunted like a wild animal, shivering in bliss and then he rolled off of Deja's body. They laid in silence, buck ass naked in her bed enjoying the aftermath of their orgasms.

Deja looked over at Jason breathing heavily through his mouth. "Bet you proud of yourself, huh?"

"As a matter of fact, I am." He smiled. "I was in rare form. You're welcome by the way."

Deja smirked. "You was aight. You got some moves."

"Yeah you know you were feeling me, *like B-AM, B-AM, B-AM, B-AM, B-AM, B-AM, B-AM, B-AM, B-AM, B-AM.*" He sang the lyrics from *Wait, The Whisper Song.*

Deja stared at his smooth chocolate skin, muscular arms, and handsome face and thought if he wasn't such a jackass she might consider being in a real relationship with him. *Oh well, I guess the dick will have to do,* she mused. She reached over for her phone and saw that the call she missed was from Danielle. She went to her menu, dialed her voicemail and listened.

"Hey Deja, when you get this message give me a call back. Ms. Sharon was rushed to Northside hospital. She's in room 374. Alright talk to you later."

Deja couldn't believe her ears. "Oh my god!"

She jumped up from the bed and Jason looked at her confused.

"What's wrong?"

"Ms. Sharon was rushed to the hospital," she told him in angst.

"Rick's mom," he clarified, hoping he wasn't hearing Deja correctly.

"Yes."

Although they didn't like one another, Jason and Danielle were there for anything Ms. Sharon needed ever since Rick left for LA. Danielle took her grocery shopping and spent time with her on weekends while Jason took her to her doctor appointments and checked in with her every other week. Just recently, she was diagnosed with insulin dependent type 2 diabetes. When he saw her last, she had a cold but didn't think it was anything too serious. News of her being rushed to the hospital made Jason feel as if he had just gotten kicked in the chest and felt partly to blame. Guilt ran through his body seeing a missed call on his phone. He never saw this coming. He got out of bed and found his clothes.

"Ah, Jason, we can't just go to the hospital smelling like this."

"Huh?" Jason looked at her confused. "Smelling like what?"

Deja tilted her head to the side and glared at him. "Sex! Let's just wash up before we go."

Jason sniffed himself and realized his body was perfumed in Deja's scent. It would be foul to show up at Ms. Sharon's bedside smelling raunchy.

"Yeah ... okay," he replied and followed Deja to the bathroom.

After taking a quick shower and getting dressed, the

two headed to the hospital.

Reunion

Rick was both physically and mentally exhausted as he drove his rental from Hartsfield Jackson Airport to Northside Hospital. As soon as he got the message that his mom had a heart attack, he got on the first flight leaving LAX to ATL. Over the years he had learned from Jason about his mother's slow decline. When he visited her for her birthday and briefly during his off season, he saw her slowing down but just attributed it to normal aging. Never did he think she would be laid up in the hospital for any reason.

When he finally arrived at the hospital he quickly made his way to her floor. His mind was racing with a million different thoughts. What was he going to do? How was he going to take care of his mother? Would he have to move back to Atlanta permanently? All of those thoughts plus a thousand more were running through his head when he opened the door to her room. The last thing he was expecting was to see, after six years, was her. His eyes meet hers and for a second they both felt every emotion they ever shared together.

"Rick." Danielle acknowledged, as she sat by his mother's bedside.

"Dani."

They both paused momentarily then his eyes darted toward mother. Slowly, he walked to the other side of the bed and took her hand. "Mom."

"She's resting," Danielle told him softly. "They have her on a lot of cardiac medication and something to stabilize her blood pressure. Her glucose levels were all over the place."

Rick looked at her with concern in his eyes.

"But they said she's stable now," she quickly added,

"just weak."

He nodded with understanding. "How long have you been here with her?"

"Since they called me yesterday evening. I guess she had us both listed as emergency contacts."

"Makes sense," he admitted. . "You're like a daughter to her."

"Almost, but I'm not."

Rick could still hear the hurt in her tone.

"I need ... I need to speak to her doctor."

Danielle nodded and pushed the call button for the nurse and asked to speak with her. A few minutes later there was a slight knock at the door.

"Come in," Rick replied.

In walked Deja followed by Jason. They were both surprised to see Rick and Danielle in the same room.

"Rick? Hey." Deja walked in and gave him a hug.

"Hey Deja. Good to see you."

"You too. Oh my god!" Her eyes went to Ms. Sharon. "How is she?"

"She's stable," Danielle responded.

"Hey bruh." Rick greeted his friend with a hug.

"Good to see you, Jason."

Jason's eyes panned over to Danielle. She greeted him with an unforgiving screw you glare and he gloated. Since Rick had been gone Danielle focused all of her animosity toward Jason whenever they saw each other. It was something Jason relished in. Truth be told, he didn't hate Danielle but always found her to be too stuck up for his liking.

"I was shocked when I heard about what happened to Ms. Sharon man." Jason moved toward the foot of her bed where he stood.

"Yeah, me too."

Danielle looked at Jason suspiciously. "How did you hear about Rick's mom?"

"What?" He asked taken off guard.

"I called and told Deja what happened so how did you find out?"

Jason paused trying to come up with a believable lie.

"Because I called him," Deja replied. "We're all family so I thought he should know. I knew you wouldn't call him."

Danielle huffed hearing the truth.

"Thank you all for coming," Rick said and looked at Danielle. "I appreciate you all looking after her."

"Well somebody has to," Danielle responded coldly.

Rick, once again, could hear the hurt in her voice. He knew the only reason she was still in the same room with him was because of her love for his mother. It didn't matter the reason, he was glad she was there. She still looked beautiful after all these years. He noticed the blonde highlights in her hair and she was no longer wearing her black rimmed glasses. She even appeared to be slightly thicker than he remembered; in all the right places. He still regretted that night at his mother's house. The door opened and in walked a young lady in scrubs.

"Hello, I'm Cathy, Ms. Westbook's nurse."

"Hi, I'm her son, Rick." He ambled toward her. "How's my mother doing?"

She nodded. "Hello Mr. Westbrook, your mother is in stable condition. May I speak to you outside for a moment?"

"Yeah." He turned and looked at his friends. "I'll be right back."

They all watched as Rick exited the room.

Deja glared at her sister. "Do you have to be so stank toward him?"

"You need to mind your business."

"And you need to get over it. His mother is lying up in the hospital for God's sake."

"I know that, Deja." Danielle became annoyed. "You were too busy to pick up the phone when I called you. I've been here all night and—"

"So do you want a gold star or something," Jason interrupted sarcastically. "You're not the only one who helps."

Danielle threw daggers with her eyes at Jason. "Shut the hell up."

"You first," he suggested, with a tilted grin.

"You're such loser, Jason."

"And you think you're better than everybody else."

"No, not everybody else, but definitely your ass."

"I rebuke you and yo edges in Jesus name!"

Danielle rolled her eyes. "You're still the same childish jackass you were in college."

"And there's that stankness again," Deja snapped, sick of her sister's attitude. "It must be so hard for you to be around people you think aren't on your level."

"I never said that."

Deja leaned forward. "You don't have too. It's written all over your bougie ass face."

Her words cut Danielle deeply. Just as World War Three was about to erupt, the door opened.

"Whoa! What the hell is going on in here?" Rick raised his voice and looked at everyone. "My Mom is right here."

Everybody felt ashamed. They knew it wasn't the time nor place.

"I'm sorry." Danielle gathered her things. "I'll come by and visit Ms. Sharon later."

"Dani … you don't have to leave."

She looked in his eyes. "Yes, I do. Excuse me."

Danielle brushed by him and left the room.

Rick looked at Deja and Jason. "Really y'all?"

~~~

ATLANTA - DEJASTARR ENTERTAINMENT, INC

A few hours later Deja went to her office. As she made her way to the main entrance she heard the familiar heavy Hemi of Kurt's Charger pull into the parking lot. She waited for him to get out. They had been friends for years. Kurt was looking fly as usual, a white tee-shirt, and black jeans. His hair was freshly cut and over the years he allowed his beard to grow out and become thick. It made him look sexier and more mature.

He smoothly approached Deja.

"Hey girl what's up?" Kurt greeted her with a hug.

"Hey, how you doing?"

He stepped back and looked her up and down.

"I'm doing almost as good as you look!"

"Boy stop!" Deja blushed. "You looking good yourself!"

"Well that's what I do," he agreed with a laugh. "Dani just called and told me about Ms. Sharon."

"Yeah, that's messed up. I was at the hospital earlier."

"How is she?"

"She's been better but I couldn't stay and look at her any longer. I already hate hospitals."

"Dani said she had a mild heart attack." He shook his head. "I never understood the term 'mild heart attack' what's so mild about your heart stopping?"

"I know right. I just saw her a few weeks ago." Deja exhaled. "I guess you never know what could happen."

"Yeah. Dani also told me what happened at the hospital between you two."

She rolled her eyes. "Oh, she did huh? Is that why you're here? To tell me how wrong I am to treat my sister like that?"

"Now you know me better than that. I just want to get your side of the story." Kurt could see Deja's mood change. "Why are you two still beefing with each other like that?

"Well," she sighed, "you know how things are between me and her."

"Not really," he answered truthfully. "I know a little about it but don't you think it's time y'all work on getting it better?"

She folded her arms. "Has Dani told you how she feels about me?"

"Yeah, she has."

"Why don't you share with me?"

Kurt sighed. "Now is not the time or place to talk about this."

"Whatever." Deja huffed.

"How about we talk later?"

"I don't wanna talk over the phone."

"Okay." Kurt looked at his watch. "Meet me at Dugan's at six. We'll talk then."

"Okay, you gonna buy me some wings too and don't be late!"

"Cool." Kurt chuckled. "Later."

He watched Deja walk to the front door. She knew Kurt would tell her the truth and that's what she needed to hear at this point. Deep down inside she was tired of fighting with her sister but honestly didn't know where to begin to fix the rift between them. She just hoped it could be fixed.

MY CURRENT SITUATION BY MARLON MCCAULSKY

Truth Hurts

ATLANTA - DUGAN'S - PONCE DE LEON AVE NE

A few hours later, across town, Kurt sat at a booth sipping on a beer. Deja walked through the door and Kurt waved her over to where he was sitting and greeted her with a hug.

"What time did we decide on," he asked jokingly.

"I'm on time, man."

"Yeah, CP time."

They both laughed.

"Whatever! I still want them wings."

"Already ordered."

"Lemon pepper?"

"Of course. I know you, girl."

Deja grinned. Kurt signaled for the waitress who came by and took her drink order. After she left Deja leaned in.

"So tell me … what has Dani been saying about me?"

Kurt took a swig of his drink and pondered his thoughts. "Well, she feels like you could be doing more with your life instead partying."

Deja rolled her eyes. "She's never taken the time to find out what I do for real. Starr and I built our company from the ground up. I work hard every day."

"I know, but you gotta admit you don't give her chance to see what you do."

"Why would I," she protested. "She judges me every chance she gets!"

Kurt gave her the side eye. "And you don't come at her too?"

Deja sighed.

"Why do you always throw the fact your father chose her Mom over yours in her face?"

"Because he did. He was there for her whenever she needed him. He paid her college tuition not mine. I had to get a job. I didn't get a free ride so she don't got no right to come at me for not finishing."

Once again Kurt gave her a knowing glare. "And how was any of that Dani's fault? That's a decision your father made and you know her mother's family got money. Even though she can be a bit abrasive at times you always go in without mercy and use your father against her. That really hurts her feelings."

"I didn't know that."

"Yes you did," Kurt said firmly taking off the kiddie gloves. "You know exactly how to get under her skin and you go hard."

Deja wanted to interrupt him but Kurt wouldn't let her.

"When she tried to reconnect with you throw up a wall and take shots at her upbringing. She's still your sister and she loves you."

Deja couldn't even deny it. She knows she could be mean to her sister and not think twice about it.

"Yeah, you're right."

"So you see why she feels the way she does?"

"Yeah, I'm a bitch," she admitted.

"I didn't say all that."

"No, but that's the truth. I'ma bitch. I can see why she hates me."

"No she doesn't." Kurt paused. "You're not exactly her bestie." They laughed together at that admission. "Trust me if she hated you, she would cut you off completely."

The waitress returned with Deja's drink and an order of twenty wings.

"Okay," she sighed. "So what can I do to make it better between us?"

"Simple, be her sister. Don't pop off at her."

Deja nodded in agreement. "Okay but she gotta stop

coming at me too. I'm tired of her judging me all the time."

Kurt nodded with understanding. "I'll talk to her."

Deja was willing to try if she was. She picked up a wing from the basket, dipped into the bleu cheese dressing and took a bite.

"So what's going on in your life, Mr. Bishop?"

"Life is good. I can't complain."

Deja pursed her lips. "So who's the lucky lady?"

Kurt took a wing and bit it. "Who says there's a lady?"

Deja grabbed another wing. "Well I guess if you're still crushing on my sister there wouldn't be anybody else huh?"

"Wow, you go right for the jugular don't you?"

She smiled. "Well like you said I'm a bitch."

"Don't put words in my mouth." He snickered. "I never called you a bitch."

"So do you still want to be with her?"

Kurt picked up a piece of chicken and ate it, contemplating his response. "I was attracted to her but that was a long time ago. If I'm being honest, Dani and I never had the chemistry to truly be good together. Gotta be both ways or it won't work."

"True." Deja nodded. "You deserve a good woman, Kurt. Not too many ones like you around."

"I always thought you could do better than some of the dudes I've seen you with. You deserve to be with a man who's gonna put you first and treat you like the real woman you are."

She smiled. "Really? Like who?"

"If you have to ask then you're really blind to what's in front of you."

Deja blushed and took another wing from the basket. They continued to eat and make small talk. This was the first time in months Deja found herself enjoying herself with a man. All she had with Jason was sex but being with Kurt felt

72

different and for the first time she started to see him in a whole new light. Kurt wasn't just a nicely dressed brother; he was also a handsome man too. Before either of them knew it two hours had passed and it was dark outside. Kurt paid for their food and walked Deja to her car.

She dug around in her purse for her keys. "Well, thanks for being honest with me, Kurt. I appreciate it."

He grinned. "I'm always gonna be honest with you, Deja."

Kurt caught her gaze then did what he had been hoping to do the whole night. He leaned closer and gently kissed her lips. Deja felt butterflies in her stomach as her lips tugged against his. He pulled away slowly.

"So … I'll call you later?" Kurt asked.

Deja was at a loss for words. She smiled and nodded. Kurt smiled and took a step back allowing her to get in her car. Deja started her engine then looked at Kurt one more time through her window. *Did that really just happen?* She smiled at him again hoping it would happen again real soon.

A Fresh Look

EAST POINT - FRESH LOOK HAIR STUDIOS

Starr was looking over the decorations she chose for the grand opening that DejaStarr was hired to organize for their client, Darnell Smith. He was referred to them by Jason. This celebration was to launch his new barbershop and hair salon opening in the Camp Creek Marketplace in East Point.

Starr was doing a walk-through making sure everything was in order, not aware that Darnell was checking her out from a distance. The fitted white shirt and dress she wore hugged her body like a second skin. She considered herself a full figured woman. She wasn't a snack, she was an entrée. It was more than her body that had him sprung; it was her personality. As cliché as that may sound it meant a lot for Darnell to not only be physically attracted to her but to enjoy being around her as well. Growing up, she wasn't always comfortable in her skin. In fact, she hated her body. It was hard being a size 14-16 while her best friend Deja barely hit a 2. It wasn't until she started dieting, working out, and loving herself that she noticed that men were always attracted to her. She just had to get over her own insecurities in order to see it. Starr turned and saw his eyes on her ass.

"I hope you like what you see, Mr. Smith."

He grinned. "Yes indeed. It looks perfect."

"Oh it does?" She quipped. "You sure there isn't anything you would like to rearrange or move?"

"Hmm ... let me see." He walked toward her. "In fact, there is something." He palmed her ass. "But, I have to do it in private."

Starr quickly looked around to make sure nobody saw them. "Hey now, careful, it doesn't look very professional for me to be seen being fondled by my client on the job."

"It's gonna be even less professional when I take you to the back room and pull them panties to the side and—"

"Hush!" She blushed and kissed him. "You are so nasty!"

"That's the only way I know how to be and you wasn't complaining about how nasty I was last night."

Starr bit her bottom lip. They had been hooking up on the low for the past week after two dates. She wasn't the type to sleep around and had only been with one other man before him but never so quickly. There was something about this man. At six foot one, Darnell had a physique like a body builder thanks to his daily regiment at the gym. Looking like a real life super Negro, it wasn't until they met professionally that they ran into each other at the same gym. A coincidence that felt more like fate than anything else. From there it went from working out, to catching a healthy meal, then eventually getting it in on her bed.

"True." She exhaled. "You're a freak."

"Takes one to know one."

She kissed him again. "What were you saying about a back room?"

Just as he was going to expand on that suggestion they both heard the door open and they broke apart.

"So, I think we're all ready to go, Mr. Smith." Starr spoke in her most professional tone as Deja walked in.

Darnell cleared his throat. "Thank you Ms. Sales. Everything looks great!"

Deja stared at them and shook her head. "Don't do that."

Starr looked at her friend. "Do what?"

Deja rolled her eyes. "The whole we're just working together, not sleeping with each other act. Cause y'all are so transparent."

"How did you know?"

"Girl, we've been friends for over sixteen years! I know you. I'm almost mad you didn't tell me sooner."

"Don't be mad at her. I didn't want to make things awkward," Darnell explained.

"Trust me, I know all about awkward situations." Deja paused and looked at her friend. "Have you told your brother about this?"

"Not yet but I will when the time is right."

"Oh, is your brother the over protective type?"

Starr looked at him. "Just a little bit."

Deja let out an uncontrollable laugh and Starr glared at her.

"Why do I feel like I'm about to walk the green mile here?" Darnell looked between the two.

"We should probably talk about my brother later okay? C'mon."

The two made their way to the back of the shop. Deja sat in one of the hairdressing chairs, took out her phone and texted a message to her sister.

⇦HEY DANI, CAN WE MEET TODAY FOR LUNCH?

⇨ OK … WHY?

⇦ I JUST NEED TO TALK TO YOU.

⇨ WHERE?

⇦TGIF. CAMP CREEK AT 12:30PM

⇨ OK.

Deja could tell by her sister's short replies that she was a bit apprehensive. She's never asked her out to lunch but she knew if there was any chance of them putting their differences to the side she had to be the one to make the first move.

MY CURRENT SITUATION   BY   MARLON MCCAULSKY

Olive Branch

Deja requested two more Jack Daniel's Honey and Sprite mixed drinks from the waitress as she waited for Danielle to show up. She quickly finished the two that the waitress brought her earlier. She needed a few drinks to relax her and put her in the right frame of mind to have this conversation. It was nearly twelve thirty so she made sure she got there fifteen minutes ahead of time. Deja knew she had a habit of being late and didn't want to start this meeting off on the wrong foot.

Danielle went inside of the restaurant and a hostess pointed to Deja at a booth in the back where she was sitting. Danielle was surprised that she was there before her. She walked to the booth and Deja greeted her with a smile. She was a little uneasy by Deja's demeanor. What was she going to say to her now? What was she up to?

"Hey," Deja greeted in a friendly tone.

Seeing two empty glasses on the table, Danielle hesitantly replied, "Hey, what's going on?"

Deja smiled and pointed in front of her. "Have a seat. I just wanted to talk to you."

"About dad's birthday party?"

"No, not that but some other things that have been on my mind lately."

Danielle grew even more wary about where this conversation was heading and her defenses were up. She knew although Deja sounded sweet now that she had a wicked tongue that could flip in a second. The waitress appeared with two drinks and placed them on the table.

"You ordered this for me?"

Deja nodded. "I know what you like."

"Do you need a few minutes before you place your

order," the waitress asked.

"Yes, please."

She left and went to her next table as Danielle took a sip of her drink. Deja was right, she did know what she liked. "That's good. So, what's on your mind?"

"Well, you and me." Deja exhaled. "Listen, I know we haven't had the best relationship over the years but I wanna try and fix it."

"You do?"

"Yes, I do."

Danielle stared at her for a second. "Why now? You've never showed much interest in wanting to have any type of relationship with me even when we were kids."

"I know ... and that's because I resented you."

"Why? What did I ever do to you other than try to be a good sister?"

Deja looked her in her eyes. "Dad chose you. He picked you and your Mom over me and for an eight year old girl that hurt."

"I never wanted it to be like that, Deja. I'm sorry you hated me all these years because of that."

"I never hated you, Dani. I was ... jealous."

Danielle paused hearing those words leave her sister's lips.

"Dani, I know the truth. I know dad was married to your Mom and my mother was his jump off, affair or whatever. And I know I was the accident that came from it." She paused feeling a little pain. "But I loved him and I just wanted him to choose us. Choose me."

Danielle's eyes softened. "But dad tried to be there for you too."

"But not the way he was there for you." Deja sighed. "You were his firstborn and I was a constant reminder of an infidelity that your Mom wanted him to forget. I resented you and as we got older I saw how much prettier and smarter you were than me and I was jealous."

"Deja, you're beautiful! Shit, I look at you sometimes and wish I could be as sexy as you are! And you're no dummy. You started your own business. It's extremely successful and you did it without a degree. "

"So why don't you ever give me credit? You constantly turn your nose up at what I do like it's not real work."

Danielle felt guilty because Deja was right. She knew she always gave her a hard time about everything.

"I'm sorry. I just see so much potential in you that I think you could do more if you tried."

"But don't you see I enjoy what I do? I'm happy and successful. Why isn't that enough for you?"

"You want the truth?" Danielle exhaled, understanding more than her sister knew. "I'm a little envious of you too."

Deja was shocked. "What? Why?"

"You're a rebel. You've always done what you wanted to do when you wanted to do it. I've always had expectations set for me by dad and my mom. I'm a lawyer because they wanted me to be. I didn't have the opportunity to figure myself out *'You have to be the best Danielle' 'Don't settle for second place' 'You're so smart! You can do better'*, she echoed the words her parents always said to her. "Do you know how it feels to have that kind of pressure on you at all times?"

"No, I guess I don't."

"So when I saw you always doing whatever you wanted to do, I felt some type of way. Plus you always come for my neck! Always calling me an over-achiever! You always made me feel like I wasn't hood enough to be your sister so I had to get back at you somehow."

Deja stared at her sister and realized they shared the same guilt.

"I'm sorry."

Danielle reached across the table and took Deja's hand. "I'm sorry too. It's a shame it took so long for us to talk like this."

"I know right." Deja giggled. "I guess we both got so used to arguing with each other that it felt normal."

"That is so fucking dysfunctional," Danielle huffed.

"And by the way, you are very sexy sis."

"No, I'm not."

"Then you must not have seen the long yearning looks from Rick."

"What?" Danielle frowned. "That's his problem."

"C'mon Dani, that was six years ago. He was young and dumb. People change."

She exhaled. "It still hurts, Deja. I'd rather not talk about him."

"Okay, so let's talk about dad's birthday dinner." They both smiled and spent the rest of lunch talking about their father. And for the first time in years they truly felt like sisters.

When Lust Isn't Enough

Deja felt good about how she had handled herself. The lunch with Danielle went well. She was able to talk like a mature woman instead of a bitter little girl with daddy issues. They both acknowledged their immature behavior to one another and it felt like they could repair their relationship. Deja decided to take more time to get to know her and not damage the growing sisterhood like she had done before. For the first time in ages they talked to each other like sisters. Even though Danielle didn't want to talk about Rick she could tell she had some unresolved feelings for him. She decided not to press the issue.

Deja had just pulled into her apartment complex when her phone chirped. She looked and saw a text from Kurt. A smile instantly spread across her face. She didn't know what it was lately but the mere thought of him made her feel some sort of way. She read his text.

⇨5:08PM- HOW R U DOING?

She replied.

⇦5:09PM- I'M GOOD! WHAT R U UP TO

⇨5:09PM- BORED AS HELL AT WORK LOL. I WAS WONDERING IF YOU'D LIKE TO GO OUT TONIGHT?

Deja smiled.

⇦5:10PM- THAT SOUNDS LIKE FUN. WHERE WE GOING?

⇨5:10PM- I GET OFF AT 6 HOW ABOUT YOU
MEET ME AT ECLIPSE DI LUNA IN
DUNWOODY ABOUT 7:30

⇦5:11PM- SOUNDS GOOD I'LL SEE U THERE

☺

⇨5:11PM- KOOL.

Deja got out of her car and went upstairs to her
apartment. Once inside, she went to her bedroom and
opened her closet door. She wanted to look good for Kurt
tonight. This was going to be her first real date in months and
was excited. After pulling out a few different jean and blouse
combinations she decided to wear a teal colored dress which
accentuated her curves along with a pair of black stilettos. She
glanced at the clock and saw it was five minutes till six so she
needed to get in the shower.

She hung the dress on the back of the closet door and
started to undress. She went into the bathroom and got in the
shower. Making sure her hair didn't get wet she turned on the
water and started to wash herself with her favorite cucumber
melon bath scrub. After a few minutes she emerged from the
shower feeling fresh. She dried herself off and pulled on the
robe she kept on the back of the bathroom door. Looking at
her toes she decided to freshen the pink polish and reached
grabbed the bottle from her vanity. Shuffling to the bed, she
sat down and just before she opened the bottle, her doorbell
rang.

"Damnit," she mumbled and glanced at the clock.
She wasn't expecting anybody and hoped it wasn't a
neighbor's kid asking for a dollar to take her trash out to the
dumpster. She went to the door, looked out of the peephole
and to her surprise saw Jason standing there. Deja exhaled.
She hadn't seen or thought about him in a few days and was a

bit pissed he decided to show up uninvited.

She opened the door. "What are you doing here?"

"Dang, no hi, hello, nice to see you?" Jason asked.

"You know you're supposed to call me before you come over."

Jason raised an eyebrow. "Why?" He tried to look around her. "You got another dude up in there?"

"No." Deja rolled her eyes. "But that's not the point. We have an understanding."

"I know. Just thought I'd stop by since I was in the neighborhood."

"In the neighborhood?" She gave him the side eye and crossed her arms in front of her. "Why and when are you just over on this side of town?"

Jason ignored the question and focused his attention on her thick thighs that were showing underneath the robe and licked his lips. "Damn you look good."

He stepped closer and caressed her ass. Deja could see the lust in his eyes and it made her smile. As annoyed as she was she couldn't help enjoying the attention he was giving her. The way he was touching her was turning her on but then she remembered she already had plans for the night.

"Jay, stop." She pulled away. "I'm going out."

"Where?"

"None of your business."

"True, it ain't my business." He tugged at the belt on her robe partially revealing her naked body underneath. "That's the business I'm here for."

A part of Deja wanted to stop him from going any further but a bigger part of her wanted him to continue. And when she felt his lips on her neck she felt another part of her get wet. He had completely opened her robe and was touching her in the ways he knew she liked. Still she knew she had to stop him.

"Jay, please," she pleaded as he pulled off her robe. "I gotta go."

"You smell good." He sniffed her neck and pushed her back on her couch. "I wonder if you taste just as good?"

He got on his knees between her legs and kissed her inner thigh. Deja bit her bottom lip watching him spread her legs further apart exposing her wetness. Deja hadn't had a man go down on her in months and wasn't going to stop him from getting a taste. She closed her eyes as Jason licked her clit slowly. His index finger pushed inside of her as he continued to lick all of her juices. Her body quivered as he consumed her and a soft moan escaped her lips. It felt like he was moving his tongue in circles and zig-zags on her clit like she was an Etch-a-Sketch. She was impressed with his tongue skills and wondered why the hell he didn't show her this talent sooner. She knew this was wrong but it felt so damn right. Jason alternated between licking and sucking her until he she erupted in pleasure in his mouth.

"Oh my gawd!" Deja cried.

"Yeah, that's what I like to hear." Jason got up, kicked off his sneakers and unbuckled his pants.

Deja watched him undress still enjoying the nut she just busted. She knew this was going to happen as soon as she let him in and felt she couldn't help herself. He was her habit—a bad habit. Jason rolled a condom on his hard penis, climbed on top of her, and pushed himself inside her wet walls. As usual the sex was rough and hot just the way she liked it.

By the time he had finally caught a nut, it was dark outside and they laid naked on the couch. Jason had drifted off to sleep but Deja was next to him with her eyes wide open. She spotted the clock on the wall which read 8:45PM. She sighed knowing she had stood Kurt up. She glanced over at Jason and shook her head. She let her libido override her good sense.

She carefully eased herself away from Jason not waking him, picked up her robe off the floor and put it on. Then she went to the bedroom and picked up her cell phone off the bed. There were two missed calls from Kurt and she checked the messages that were left.

"Hey Deja, I'm here at Eclipse di Luna. You on that CP time again? Call me and let me know how far away you are. Bye."

She checked the next message.

"Well, it's 8:25 … guess you ah… guess you got held up huh? Well I'm gonna go … I guess I'll talk to you later."

Deja exhaled, she could hear the disappointment in his voice. She really wanted to see him tonight and felt like a jerk. She wanted to call him back but then thought to herself what was she going to say? *Sorry, I stood you up, I was too busy getting my pussy ate?* That wasn't going to work. She locked her phone. So much for her promise to be a better friend she thought.

She heard Jason yawning and it pissed her off that he was still there. She got up off the bed and walked into the living room. He still sprawled out naked on the couch with a grin on his face. She picked up his clothes off the floor and threw them at him.

"Hey … what you do that for?"

"It's time for you to go," she told him flatly.

"C'mon man … just let me rest." He pushed the clothes off of him.

She picked them back up and threw them on him again.

"Get yo ass up, Jay!" Deja barked. "You can sleep at your own damn house. You know the rules no spending the night."

He sat up and glared at her. "Damn man … aight."

She stood and watched as he got dressed.

Jason glanced at her staring at him. "You mad cuz I made you miss going wherever you were going tonight?"

Deja huffed and didn't reply.

"You acting like you didn't enjoy yourself."

"I did, but you know you're only supposed to come if I call you. What if Dani was here?"

Jason fastened his belt and walked over to her. "Alright ma."

He kissed her and walked to the front door.

"Well call me soon, cuz man," he turned, looked her up and down and grinned, "you got that good-good!"

Jason opened the door and left. Normally Deja would feel good having a man complement her like that but this time she didn't really care. As good as the sex was with Jason it just didn't give her the same feeling she had with Kurt the other night. Maybe just lust alone wasn't enough anymore.

Big Brother is Watching

EAST POINT - FRESH LOOK HAIR STUDIOS

Miguel's ode to love *"Adorn"* filled the air as folks swayed and drank cocktails inside Darnell's new shop. From the outside looking in it looked like the opening of the dopest new club in Atlanta. DejaStarr Entertainment had pulled off another successful grand opening. Even though it was nine o'clock on a Friday night the hype and promotion would carry on until the official store opening Saturday morning.

Darnell could not have been more pleased with the turnout for the event. It was well worth the money he invested. What was an unexpected bonus was his newfound relationship with the latter half of the promotional duo, Starr. His eyes were fixated on her. The white dress she chose for the event fit her like a second skin and showed all of her luscious curves. Images of her full figure on top of him danced in his head as he remembered their last encountered a few nights ago. He was officially sprung. Starr moved through the crowd and stopped at the makeshift bar that was set up in the back. Darnell walked up behind her.

"Whatcha drinking, ma?"

She turned around and smiled. "Budweiser."

"Good choice."

"Are you enjoying your party, Mr. Smith?"

He nodded. "Yes I am, Ms. Sales. I'm going to enjoy the after party even more."

"The after party? When did you arrange that?"

"Just a few seconds ago and only one other person is invited." He leaned and whispered in her ear. "Just you me in my bed."

She blushed. "Is there a dress code?"

He placed his hand on her hip. "Yeah, you're only allowed to wear them heels."

She leaned in close, her lips nearly touching his earlobe. "I like that."

As they were in the middle of the flirtatious exchange Kima and Mike walked over to them.

"Hey Starr!" Kima announced loud enough to get her attention.

She turned toward her. "Oh, hey y'all!"

Mike glared at them both not thrilled at how close this strange man was to his sister.

"Hey," he said dryly.

"This is Darnell. He's the owner of Fresh Look," Starr introduced. "Darnell, this is my brother, Mike and his wife, Kima."

"Nice to meet you both." He extended his hand and Kima shook it.

Mike looked at his hand for as second as if debating to shake it or break it until he felt a quick sharp elbow from his wife. He shook his hand. Darnell could feel the tension as an awkward silence fell over them.

"You have a beautiful place," Kima acknowledged.

"Thank you. This is the fulfillment of a lifetime dream for me."

Kima smiled. "Congratulations! The party is a great way to kick things off."

"Well, I can't take credit for it." He looked at Starr. "DejaStarr did all the hard work tonight."

Darnell gazed in Starr's eyes and she blushed. Mike watched the silent non-verbal exchange between the two and didn't like it one bit.

"So you do hair? Perms and whatnots?"

Both Kima and Starr cut their eyes at Mike.

"I cut. My girl, Niecy, handles the ladies."

"Yo, Darnell!" Jason yelled. "Wus up my ninja!"

He turned and smiled. "Let me go see what this fool wants." He looked at Starr. "I'll talk to you later."

"Okay." She winked.

Darnell made his way through the crowd over to his friend.

"So those two are close?" Kima asked, watching the two men then turned back to Starr.

"Yeah, Jason is the one who referred him." She took a swig of her beer.

"Oh he did huh?" Mike countered with a frown on his face. "You two were pretty chummy with each other. What's going on?"

"He's my client, Mike, and a very nice man."

"Yeah, I bet he is." He squinted. "How well do you know him?"

She sighed. "I know him very well."

"He doesn't sound like he's from Atlanta."

"Because he's not." Starr folded her arms across her chest. "Anything else you wanna know?"

Before Mike could continue his interrogation, Kima stepped in.

"Ah honey, can you get me a drink? Pineapple and Malibu please."

Mike stared at his sister, then at his wife, sighed, and went to the bar.

"Thanks girl."

"No problem." Kima grinned. "But I know you and Mr. Sexual Chocolate are more than just business associates."

"What?" Starr blushed. "What do you mean?"

"Girl, it's written all over your face."

"I'll tell you what's going on soon but for right now can you keep Mike off my back?"

"You know I got you, girl."

Mike returned with his wife's drink.

Starr gave her a hug. "Let me go find Deja!"

Kima giggled. "Later."

Starr quickly moved through the crowd. Kima stepped in front of her husband and took the cup from his hand. "Thank you."

Mike tried to go around her but she blocked him.

"Hey, I need to talk to Starr for a second."

"No you don't., Kima said frankly. "You need to back off and let her be."

"I wanna know—"

She cut him off. "You were rude."

"What?"

"To Darnell. This is his party and you were rude, Michael."

He sighed. He could tell there was something going on between Darnell and his sister. Something he didn't like but he also knew when Kima called him by his first name she was annoyed with him. After six years of marriage, Mike knew this was a battle he didn't want to fight.

"I'm sorry, okay?"

Kima placed her hand on her husband's cheek in a gentle caress. "Mike, when Starr is ready to talk to you she will."

"Okay, okay." He glanced over at Darnell still talking to Jason. "We'll talk soon."

Kima shook her head and sipped her drink. She knew her husband was a gentle giant with a big heart but when it came to his sister he could be an overbearing prick. Even if she liked it or not. But she also knew he could easily be distracted if given the right bait. She wrapped her arms around his neck.

"Hey, you know how you've wanted to expand our family?"

"Yeah." He smiled.

"Well, I think now might be a good time," she whispered. "I'm ovulating."

His eyes lit up. "Really? You mean right now as in you're ready?"

"Yes." She kissed his lips.

"Well look at the time, I'm ready to go. How about you?"

She chuckled. "Lead the way, baby."

Old Wounds

SANDY SPRINGS - NORTHSIDE HOSPITAL

She was the first woman he ever loved. His first kiss came from her. No matter how bad he acted she loved him. As he looked at her beautiful face he wished there was something more he could do than just hold her hand. Rick had been by his mother's side for the past two days. He felt an overwhelming sense of undeserved guilt for not being there for her. When, in truth, he could have been standing right next to her and been just as powerless to stop it. Rick's stomach growled. He had been dining from the vending machine on a regular basis. Cokes, M&M's, and Doritos were in his daily rotation. His stomach grumbled again.

"You should eat something, baby," his mother articulated in a soft tone.

"Mom?" Rick's eyes lit up.

"Um huh," she responded softly.

"How do you feel?"

"Tired."

"Just rest. Anything you need, I'm right here."

"Sounds like you need a good meal." The corners of her mouth turned upward and she patted his hand.

Rick smiled. "I'll be alright, I got some Funnions I'm about to get into. I'm so happy you're awake. The doctor said you'll be very tired for a while."

"How long ... have I been here?"

"Two days."

"You came all the way from LA?"

"Of course I did. As soon as I got the call I was on the first thing here."

He leaned in and kissed her forehead.

"Richard..."

"Yes Mom?"

"You need to go eat something."

94

"Mom." He shook his head, "Don't worry about me."

She exhaled. "You need to take care of yourself."

"Well right now I'm taking care of you. I was so scared when Dani told me what happened."

Sharon smiled. "Danielle? She was here?"

"Yeah, she was the first one here."

"She's such a good girl." She coughed.

Rick quickly grabbed the pitcher next to her bed and poured a little water in a cup. He raised the head of her bed then held the cup at her lips as she slowly took a few sips then rested her head against the pillow. Rick gazed at her with concern. He had never seen his mother so weak. It was so strange to see her like this. If he could give her his heart he would without a second thought.

"Take it easy, mom. Rest."

She nodded and looked at her handsome son. She could see how worried he was and knew he would do anything to help her. Even if it meant neglecting his own happiness. That's why she never told him about her declining health over the last few years. The diabetes she had recently been dealing with became worse. Her insulin had to be increased and her most recent bout with a cold a month ago had further compromised her health. It threw her body off, making her more susceptible to anything. After a few minutes they heard a knock on the door.

"Come in," Rick spoke up.

The door opened and in walked Danielle. Both Rick and Sharon smiled. She was dressed in blue faded jeans and purple button down blouse. Her long curly hair hung down around her shoulders. It had been so long since he seen her dressed down and he liked it. Natural. Unfiltered. Beautiful.

Danielle gazed at her former fiancé. She knew he would still be here. His beard had grown in more since she last saw him two days ago. He was also in need of a haircut. He looked understandably rough around the edges. What man wouldn't be sleeping in a hospital room next to his sick mother? Her eyes then went to Ms. Sharon, the woman she loved like a second mother. She was relieved that she was awake.

"Hey, there's my girl." She smiled and moved toward the bed. "How are you feeling?"

"I'm okay."

They knew that was a polite lie.

"I was so worried. Has the doctor been in to see you yet?"

"Not yet." Rick answered.

Danielle looked at him. Somehow even through his roughness he was still handsome. She wanted to ignore him but looking at his sleep deprived eyes she couldn't be mean.

"Oh, how are you?"

"I'm okay now." He looked at his mother. "Somebody had me worried."

"I'll be okay. I just … I just need to get my strength back."

Rick took her hand. "You will, Mom. I'ma make sure you do."

Danielle could see the love and concern in his face for his mother. Although she knew it wouldn't be an easy road to making a full recovery, she would be there every step of the way for Ms. Sharon. Her eyes then caught the small trash can near the bed filled with soda cans and candy wrappers. She could tell Rick had been eating crap for the last two days. As much as she didn't care about his well-being she knew if he wasn't strong he would be no good for his mother.

Danielle looked at him. "Rick, have you eaten anything decent?"

"Ah …"

"No he hasn't," his mother answered.

"I can answer for myself, Mom."

"He hasn't showered either."

"Ma!"

"Richard, my heart might be weak but my nose is

working quite fine."

"Really, this is the thanks I get?" He shook his head.

A smile crept across Danielle's face seeing their exchange.

"Danielle, can you please take Richard to get something to eat?"

Rick's jaw dropped. "Ma, I don't want to impose—"

"No problem, Ms. Sharon," she interrupted and looked at him. "C'mon, let's grab a bite in the cafeteria."

Rick was shocked at how quickly Danielle agreed.

He looked at his mom who was smiling. "I'll still be here when you get back," she mused.

Danielle leaned over and kissed Ms. Sharon's cheek. "I'll be back to check on you."

Sharon continued to smile as the two exited the room. It had been her wish for them to get back together again. Even though the pain Danielle felt was deep, Sharon knew time healed old wounds.

The two walked in silence down the hallway. Rick wanted to say something but given the fact Danielle hadn't thrown any daggers at him, he decided to keep the peace. After a quiet ride down the elevator they both went to the cafeteria and got some food. Rick got a double cheese burger, chicken nuggets, fries, and a Coke. Danielle opted for a grilled chicken salad and apple juice. Rick didn't realize how hungry he was until he dove into his food with no regard for human life. Back in the day, Danielle would have called him out but given their current situation decided to let him slide.

He looked up at her. "Thanks for lunch."

"No problem."

"So how have you been?"

She poked at her salad then tasted it. "Fine."

Rick nodded. "Mike told me you made partner at the firm. Congratulations! I always knew you would. You've always been so driven. Focused. Shit, I bet in a few years you'll be running the joint! I can see—"

"What are you doing?" She cut him off.

"Ah, just making conversation."

"Why? This isn't a date."

"I know it's not. I was just trying to catch up with you. It's been a while."

"There's no need to. I'm just doing your mother a favor and making sure you eat something. Nothing has changed between us."

Rick looked at her. "Dani, I'm sorry. I know what I did to you was wrong. I was scared. I know it's not an excuse but I didn't want to make such a big commitment to you and not be sure. You gotta believe me I never wanted to hurt you."

She glared at him.

"You feel better now? You got that off your chest?"

"Dani …"

"Believe it or not I got over you a long time ago. I just don't like you." She got up from the table. "Finish your meal, then go home and clean yourself up. I'll stay with your Mom and once you come back I'll leave."

Danielle picked up her salad and walked away. Rick sat back in his chair and watched her leave. This wasn't the first time he apologized. Years ago he sent letters and reached out to her on social media only to be ignored. He always thought that if she could see how sorry he was, look in his eyes and hear his voice that maybe she could forgive him. Obviously he underestimated the level of *'I hate your guts'* she had built up over the years. Maybe some wounds don't ever heal completely.

MY CURRENT SITUATION   BY   MARLON MCCAULSKY

#101

Deja needed to get some advice on how to deal with the Kurt and Jason situation. She knew she couldn't go to Danielle; she hated Jason, and besides they were just starting to reconnect as sisters and didn't want anything to deter it. Starr was her best friend but her experience with men was limited so the only other person she felt she could talk to was Kima. She always went to her for advice over the years.

After her run in with Jason yesterday evening she still felt bad for standing Kurt up but had no idea what to say to him. She thought perhaps Kima could give her a bit of insight on what to do next. Once Deja arrived, the mother of two was preparing dinner. Deja sat at the table watching her move around the kitchen like a chef on the Food Network. Kima could tell by Deja's face that whatever was going on in her life was weighing heavily on her mind.

"Why you look so depressed?"

Deja looked at her with a perplexed expression painted on her face. "I do?"

"Yes. What's going on?"

"I'm just trying to figure out how to deal with the men in my life." She sighed.

Kima was curious whom she was referring to. She knew Deja was damn near like a dude when it came to dating. She always had men chasing after her but catching feelings was something she never did. Who could have possibly got past her defenses?

"Men? As in plural?"

"Yeah."

"Okay, in what way?"

Deja debated if should tell Kima about her and Kurt.

She didn't want Danielle to know about their connection because she had no idea how she felt about him. Although Kurt confirmed they were just friends she still didn't want to be caught up in another situation with her sister.

"I wanna tell you something I've been keeping on the low for a while."

Kima put down her spoon and sat at the table with Deja. "Trust me, no one knows how to keep a secret like me."

"Okay." Deja nodded. "Well, you know me and Kurt are friends right?"

Kima leaned closer. "Yeah."

"We ran into each other the other day then hung out at Dugan's later on that night. I don't know how it happened but we kissed each other in the parking lot."

"What?" Kima grinned. "Wow! I ... I didn't see that one coming."

"I know, neither did I but it happened and I liked it."

"Okay, well that's good right?"

"Yeah, but then we were supposed to go out for dinner Monday night and I kinda stood him up," she confessed regrettably.

"Why?"

Deja sighed. "I'm not proud of myself but before I could get dressed to meet him," she paused and diverted her eyes from Kima's, "Jason came over unannounced and we ... did some thangs."

Kima's mouth fell open with surprise. "Oh my gawd! You and Jason?"

"There is no me and Jason. He just stops by and we fuck."

"Wow, Dani would lose her shit if she knew about you two."

"This is why I keep it private. I haven't talked to Kurt since. I really don't know what to say to him," Deja explained. "He just caught me at a bad time and he ..."

"And he what?" Kima smiled.

"His tongue game is on point."

Kima laughed and gave her a high five. "Yes girl! I know you made sure he got a mouth full!"

"Every last drop," she cosigned with a laugh.

"I know that's right! I can't stand when a man is wasting all my good juices. Get it off ya chin and in your mouth! Most of these fools need to take a class on pussy eating one-o-one."

Deja giggled at her comment. "I agree; but still, I really wanna get to know Kurt better. I really like him."

"Well, you gonna have to call him and make up a good story why you stood him up."

"Yeah, I know."

~~~

THE PARK

Deja knew a phone call wouldn't satisfy her. She wanted Kurt to know how genuinely sorry she was so after she left Kima's house she drove out to the park on Norcross where she knew he liked to play basketball ever afternoon. She pulled up, got out of her car and spotted him playing a pickup game with some guys. He was taking the ball up the court and Deja was impressed. It was probably the first time she ever saw him without a blazer and was mesmerized with his well-defined frame in sports gear. Out of all the years she had known him she never looked at him in this light.

She slowly walked to the side of the basketball court. Kurt took the ball to the hole blowing past the guy guarding him and made an easy layup. He then turned and saw Deja standing to the side of the court watching him. He was surprised to her here of all places.

He turned and looked at the other guys on the court. "Hey, give me a minute."

He walked toward her. Deja could feel her heart rate increase as he got closer. She could see the beads of sweat rimming his brow and twinkling down his muscular frame. Deja found herself aroused by his masculinity.

"Hey," Kurt greeted.

"Hi," Deja responded shyly.

"What are you doing here?"

"I came to see you." She begin fidgeting. "I … I wanted to apologize for leaving you hanging the other night."

Kurt nodded. "What happened?"

Deja swallowed hard thinking of her answer. "I got scared," she lied. "I just … I was afraid of …"

"Afraid of what? Me?"

"I was afraid that if you got to know the real me you probably wouldn't like me," she said softly.

Kurt was surprised by her words. "Wouldn't like you? Deja I've known you for years. I think I know you pretty well."

"You sure about that? Cause I can be a real bitch when I wanna be."

Kurt chuckled. "I know, but that doesn't change the fact that I wanna get to know the real you even better."

Deja smiled hearing him say that. She was relived she hadn't completely blown it with him and wanted to get to know him better as well. She couldn't help it as her eyes trailed down his hard abs to his waistline. His basketball shorts just stopping above his nether region and she only imagined what other hard member was underneath those shorts. She snapped herself out of her nasty daydream and refocused on his face. Kurt could see the way she was looking at his body and knew she liked what she saw.

"So do you think you can forgive me?" She waited for an answer and was relieved when he smiled.

"Depends on how you wanna make it up to me."

Deja blushed at his flirtatious remark.

"How about we go out to dinner tomorrow night, my

treat," she offered.

Kurt smiled and nodded. "Sounds good to me, I know a good spot we can go."

"You can come over to my place and pick me up."

"Yeah. Text me later."

"Okay, I'll let you get back to your game now … don't wanna get the boys mad at you," she joked.

Kurt glanced back at them. "Forget them fools."

Deja laughed and headed back to her car. Kurt stood and watched in awe as how thick Deja's ass was in skinny jeans. She had the kind of walk that could literally stop a man dead in his tracks. The guys on the basketball court were frozen as they watched her hips swish from side to side with each step. Deja glanced back and saw Kurt looking at her ass and smiled. If he liked what he saw now he was gonna fall out tomorrow night.

MY CURRENT SITUATION   BY   MARLON MCCAULSKY

The Set Up

UNION CITY - MIKE & KIMA'S HOUSE

Kima invited Danielle and Deja over for dinner. Normally Starr would have been included but she already had plans with Darnell and inwardly, she was relieved. She didn't want the night to be awkward with Mike giving him the third degree. That was a battle for another day. Besides, she had an ulterior motive. Given Danielle's recent moodiness because of Rick's return she decided to do something to change it.

The sisters arrived at Kima's. Danielle parked behind a red and white Mini Cooper which was parked next to Mike's black Toyota SUV. Both Danielle and Deja exited her car, went to the front door, and rang the doorbell. A few seconds later Kima opened the door.

"Hey!" She happily greeted them with a hug. "You both look so cute!"

"So do you," Danielle replied, admiring the short tank dress she wore. "I see why Mike stay on it!"

"True!" Kima winked and let them in.

"Something smells good," Deja declared. "What you cooking?"

"Nothing fancy. Just Ox tails and butter beans."

"Oooh have I told you how much I love you?" Danielle confessed.

Kima led them to the living room where they spotted two handsome men on the couch watching TV. Both of them stood up as they walked in and Mike wrapped his arm around his wife.

"Hey y'all! I can't believe it."

"Can't believe what?" Danielle quizzed, looking around.

"You two actually came here together and there's no

106

bloodshed."

"Shut up, Mike," she retorted.

"This is our friend, Kenneth," Kima introduced with a smile.

"Hello," he said in a sexy and smooth tone. "Most people call me Ken."

He stood about six feet even with broad shoulders and a caramel brown complexion. Danielle knew right away this was a set up on her friend's part. If Ken wasn't such a good looking brother she would have been annoyed.

"Ken, these are my friends, Danielle and her sister, Deja." Kima smiled.

He stepped closer and gently shook Deja's hand then Danielle's. Ken took in her lovely face and sexy body then smiled at her. "Nice to meet you both."

Deja knew even though he said 'both' he was really speaking to Danielle. In the past Deja would have felt some type of way if a dude paid her sister more attention than her but because of her budding relationship with Kurt she didn't mind. Ken was fine but she could tell by the smile on Danielle's face she was feeling him. Deja was glad because her sister needed some male attention.

"Thank you," Danielle replied not wanting to let go of his hand too fast.

Kima gleamed, seeing the obvious attraction between the two. Everything was going as planned. "Well why don't you all go into the dining room. I'll get dinner plated."

"Let me get that for you," Ken offered pulling out the chair for Danielle. He then sat across from her taking in her beauty. Danielle could feel his eyes on her but didn't mind it. Mike, being the outgoing kind of man he was, made small talk and cracked jokes making everybody laugh until Kima emerged from the kitchen with the food. As usual, her cooking was delicious. Danielle and Deja loved every bite and had seconds. The conversation at the table was light but the non-verbal communication between Danielle and Ken was evident. The way they exchanged glances, the way she would play with her hair and the way he licked his lips enjoying his meal spoke volumes. After they were done eating everyone retreated to the living room to relax. Mike turned on the TV and flipped to the Lakers vs. Clippers playoff game that was about to start.

"I hope LeBron just hurries up and knock them off," Mike mentioned to Ken.

"Bruh you better kill that noise!" Ken bellowed. "This ain't Cleveland and there's a new sheriff in town and his name is Kawhi."

Mike gave him a side eye. "What's a sheriff to a king? A baller to a legend? Kawhi is nice but King James is better."

"Boooo," Danielle interjected. "LeBron sucks."

Ken got up from the recliner and gave Danielle a fist bump. "And you know this maaaan!"

"Whatever, you weren't saying all that when he won two back to back championships."

"Ah, what happened that last year in Miami though?" Danielle reminded Mike.

"They lost cause he's a choker!" Ken added grabbing his neck.

"They didn't lose because he choked," Mike shot back. "Hell, he was carrying the whole damn team! The Spurs just had a better team that year. Well after they destroy the Clippers tonight we'll see what you got to say."

Ken sat next to Danielle on the couch. "Yeah, we'll see."

Danielle made note of the smooth way Ken changed seats to be closer to her. She liked his style; not over the top in flirting but he was clearly showing his interest in talking with her.

Deja enjoyed seeing the chemistry between them and decided to excuse herself, leaving the pair alone.

Danielle watched her sister head toward the kitchen.

"Baby," Kima called out. "Can you help us in here

please?"

Danielle picked up on what was happening.

"Huh? Right now?"

Kima stood at the doorway and gave him a knowing look. "Yes, right now."

He was oblivious to what was happening until his wife slyly nodded at Danielle and Ken. "I'll be back in a minute."

Sitting for a few seconds in silence watching the NBA pre-game show, Ken chuckled.

"What's so funny?" Danielle glanced at him.

"Them. I guess it's kinda obvious what they're up to."

"Yeah." She smiled. "I guess it is."

"I should have known Kima was setting me up when she told me to wear something nice tonight." He shook his head.

"Well, she got me good," Danielle confirmed. "So you're single?"

"Yeah. I just got out of a relationship a couple of months ago."

"Did it end badly?"

Ken shook his head. "No. We were together for about five month. We were just heading in two different directions in life. She was really more into her career than us so we just decided to be friends."

Danielle nodded. "So you wanted to be more serious?"

"I guess, yeah. She's a third year medical student. Trying to juggle that and a relationship just didn't work for her."

"Oh, are you a doctor too?"

"No, I'm a Cardiac Sonographer at Northside, how about you?"

As much as she's been at Northside over the last three days Danielle was surprised she hadn't run into him.

"I'm an attorney at Gant & Associates."

Ken's eyebrows raised. "Impressive!"

"Thank you."

"So how long have you and Kima been friends?"

"Oh gosh, since junior high. Besties, actually," she kindly informed.

"Cool." Ken looked at her. It was just unbelievable how attractive she was to him. Normally he would hate being set up on a blind date but not this time. "So Danielle ..."

"You can call me Dani," she offered. "Everybody else does." She was feeling a little bit more comfortable with him.

"Okay, so Dani, before I continue to drag this out any further, let me ask you, are you single?"

"Yes, I am."

"No crazy dude wearing footies coming to the club trying to find you?"

She laughed at his joke. "Hell no!"

"Cool, so would you mind if I called you sometime? Maybe we could get to know each other a little bit better."

Danielle stared at Ken for a second debating if it was a good idea to take this any further considering Rick had been on her mind ever since he's been back. Even though Ken seemed like a great guy was he going to be just another asshole to her in the end? She promised herself the next guy she met would have to deal with her on her terms. If Ken couldn't understand or if she saw any signs of bullshit she had no problem cutting him loose with no remorse.

Danielle took out her cell, unlocked it, and gave it to him. "I'd like that."

Ken showed off his million dollar smile, dialed his number into her phone and called his cell. He handed it back to her.

"What's your last name, Ken?"

"Hayes, Ken Hayes." He extended his hand to her. Danielle smiled and shook it. "Danielle Queen."

"Nice to meet you Ms. Queen. You don't mind if I

run a background check on you?"

Danielle laughed out loud. "What?"

"I'm just saying, you cute and everything but you could be crazy! I'm just trying not to get cut," he joked.

"Well," she shrugged, "you better not give me a reason to cut you."

"Ahhh, see there," he pointed at her, "those are the tale tell signs of a crazy deranged sista."

"Whatever! You just better not be crazy!"

Ken smiled at her and Danielle couldn't fight the smile that spread across her face. Despite the undeniable chemistry she felt with Ken she didn't want to get too far ahead of herself.

Nights Like This

There's no way to explain why certain people make you feel a certain type of way. Never in Starr's life had she felt this way about a man. She'd been in love before but this was different. Her first love, Tariq, was special but being as young as they were and with their lives going in different directions it didn't last. But when she met Darnell it was different. Being with him felt more natural than any relationship she had in the past and their open communication was nothing like she had before. She was now a woman who knew who she was as a person and knew exactly what she wanted. Darnell respected her mind and body but most importantly, he made her feel loved.

For weeks they had been keeping their relationship on the low but now that their business was done, there was no reason for them to hide it. So when Darnell asked her to hang out at Jason's Lounge, she was good to go. This was a familiar spot where she liked to party with Deja. And being personal friends with the owner meant they got the VIP treatment. Jason opened his club four years ago and business was booming ever since. As soon as they walked through the doors, Jason spotted the couple and did a double take. He knew Starr since she was a little girl and, out of respect for his boy Mike, never gave much thought to the idea of hooking up with her no matter how attractive she became over the years. That, plus the fact Mike would probably rip his head off, kept her off limits.

He knew his boy was a notorious playa. With Rick living in LA for the past six years, Darnell became Jason's his wingman on many of nights and his sexual exploits rivaled his. He was surprised to see Starr with him. She wasn't the type of girl Darnell normally dated. Jason knew he liked his

112

women young and dumb but Starr was neither. She was smart, funny, and an all around good girl. Jason made his way over toward the couple.

"Well, well, well, will you look at you two. What the hell is in this Georgia water," Jason chided with a smile on his face.

Starr laughed at him. "I don't know, Jay. What did you put in it?"

Darnell gave his friend a man hug.

Jason gave Starr a hug also. "I gotta say, when I recommended DejaStarr to you I didn't expected you to take advantage of all their benefits."

Darnell shook his head. "Boy, you stupid."

"Well, I know for fact he isn't the only one getting benefits," she purposely implied and raised a perfectly arched brow. Jason grinned knowing what she was referring to. She was after all Deja's best friend. If anybody would know, it would be her.

"Touché. So I guess you've met Mike?"

"Yeah, I have ... briefly."

Starr stared at Jason. "And I would appreciate if you'd use some discretion the next time you speak to my brother."

"Always Starr Bright. Do you mind if I speak to my boy real quick?"

"No, not at all." She looked at Darnell. "I'll be at the bar, bae."

"Alright." He gave her a kiss.

As she walked away, he admired her body in the little black dress she chose for their evening.

"So, what's going on bruh? You two for real?" Jason asked.

"As real as it gets. There's something special about her."

"You ain't lying about that. She's a good girl. If you serious about her, don't mess it up."

Darnell nodded. "Jay, what's up with her brother? I

met the man once and he was throwing all kinds of shade my way."

"Don't take it personal, bruh. Mike's a good dude but when it comes to his sister he goes into asshole mode quick."

"Damn, I know some dudes are protective of their sister and all but she's a grown woman."

"Their dad died when she was young so Mike kinda filled that role. Don't worry, I'll talk to him. Let him know, you a good dude like me."

Darnell shook his head and laughed. "Lord if you say that he'll put her in the witness protection program and I'll never see her again!"

While the two men caught up, Starr signaled for the bartender.

"A Long Island Iced Tea please."

The bartender nodded and Starr leaned against the bar watching everyone rush to the floor when the DJ played a new Drake tune. As she waited, she suddenly felt some hot breath on her shoulder.

"Hey lil' momma whatcha drankin'?"

Starr turned her head and saw him. He was a medium built brother dressed like the average wannabe thug. But what turned her off immediately was, not that he was obviously drunk and his breath smelled like hot garbage, it was the long dreadlocks that cropped his face. Instantly, she didn't want any parts of him and didn't want to give him any hope.

"I already ordered a drink," she replied.

"Oh that's good, let me get your next one."

"Nah, that's alright I'm good, playa."

He stutter stepped. "But I can make you better. Come dance wit me ma."

"Nah, that's okay." She shook her head. "I'm here with somebody."

She turned around as the bartender returned with her drink and took a sip. Thinking her admirer had taken the cue and moved on, she was surprised to still see him standing behind her. "What?"

"I'm just waiting on you, ma!"

Starr frowned. "Waiting on me for what?"

"To stop playin' and get with this real man right here. C'mon ma don't be shy." He took her wrist and Starr snatched her arm back.

"Don't ever grab me like that again! I told yo ass I wasn't interested! Now fuck off!"

Starr's voice got the attention of everybody in the immediate area and all eyes were on them.

He mean mugged her. "You see, this why you bitches ain't shit! Cause you don't recognize when a real man steps to you! You dumb ass bitch!"

She took a second to absorb what the drunken fool said to her. By nature she was a sweetheart but that didn't mean she couldn't go from zero to one hundred real quick.

"I ain't shit? Fool, yo momma ain't shit! Yo sister, grandmother, auntie, and cousin ain't shit if I ain't! And yo breath smell like dog shit! You need to ask the bartender for glass of Listerine on the rocks you fuckin' loser!"

People within earshot laughed and the dude was embarrassed. He was not going to let her humiliate him without being put in her place. Just as he was pulling back to punch her in the face he felt himself getting yanked backward by his collar like a rag doll and thrown to the floor. He looked up and saw Darnell's hulking frame standing over him. Any ideas he had about hitting Starr went out the window.

"Get the fuck outta here!" Darnell growled.

He quickly got to his feet and drunkenly scurried away.

"Well aren't you my hero," Starr crooned.

Darnell turned and looked at her. "You know how I do," he assured with ease.

Seeing her man in action turned her on. Starr smiled and took another sip of her drink. They spent the next half hour at the bar drinking and enjoying each other's company. The connection they formed over the past month was stronger than either had expected. After downing her second Long Island, Starr wanted to dance and was eager to feel Darnell's against her body.

She slid off of the bar stool and extended her hand. "Come with me."

He took it and followed her onto the dance floor. The DJ was playing "*When We*" by Tank and Starr started whining her hips to the beat while grinding on him. It didn't take long for her to feel the excitement growing in his jeans. Darnell rubbed his hands all over her body touching her bare thighs and ass like they were alone in his bedroom. She enjoyed the feeling of his strong hands on her delicate body. Starr turned around and put her chest against his and he firmly planted his hands on her ass. Jason stood from a distance watching how freaky Starr was. It was a side he had never seen of her and was amused by it all.

"You ready to get out of here?" Darnell whispered in her ear.

"And go where?" She gently caressed his back.

"Somewhere special."

Starr gently pulled away from him and took his hand. They walked off the dance floor and headed toward the exit.

~~~

MIDTOWN - THE GEORGIAN TERRACE

Driving down Peachtree Street in Atlanta is a mixture of history and modern day achievement. Darnell was born and spent most of his childhood in Jackson, Mississippi. He relocated to Atlanta five years ago and even now he was still in awe of the Midtown area. Sitting in his black GMC Terrain SUV he loved seeing the flashing lights of the fabulous Fox Theater.

The musical Wicked was playing tonight. He thought

it would be nice to catch a show with Starr before it left. He turned his truck into the hotel entrance of Georgian Terrace. Having been open since 1911 it was considered an icon amongst Atlanta hotels. It was probably the most elegant he's ever stayed at with its floor to ceiling windows, crystal chandeliers and white marble columns. Starr was surprised by how far Darnell had gone for her. They made their way up to the 22nd floor to the luxury suite he reserved for the weekend.

As soon as the suite door closed they were all over one another. Kissing like they were long lost lovers. There were no need for words; they both knew what they wanted. Darnell slid his hands underneath her short dress and cupped her ass cheeks and caressed her flesh. He pulled her thong to the side and put his hand between her thighs.

"Damn, you wet," he whispered.

"You know how I do." Starr echoed his words from earlier.

He rubbed his fingers back and forth over her clit making her moan. Soon, her pool of warm sticky juices were dripping off his fingers and he was ready to jump in.

Darnell led her to the master bedroom and once inside, Starr sat back on the bed while he removed her bra and thong. She opened her legs wide. Without being asked, he went head first between her thighs and tasted her, licking her clit like it was the sweetest thing he ever enjoyed.

Starr fell back against the bed enjoying the sensations he was giving her. She had never had a man go down on her the way he did. She had only been with Tariq but he wasn't as good of a lover as Darnell was. She never insisted it either but he unlocked her inner freak with his tongue and she loved it. She clasped her legs around his back then put her hands on the back of his head giving him more of her to taste. Darnell was damn near drowning but he loved it.

"Ah … ah … Shit! That's it! Oh yes, oh my … Darnell!" Starr yelled and came in his mouth.

Darnell drank her juices like sweet honey. Finally, he

pulled away from her vice grip and stood up. She looked heavenly, lying naked on the bed. Her vagina glistened, inviting him to get inside of her moist walls.

"Damn, you're beautiful."

She smiled. "And I'm all yours."

He pulled a gold packaged condom from his pocket, and undressed. Starr finally saw the main attraction and was amazed by how long his manhood stood. Darnell rolled the condom on and climb on top of her. He kissed her breasts and rubbed his shaft up and down her wetness. But before he could slide in she stopped him.

"Wait."

Darnell looked at her confused. "Huh?"

"That's not the way I want it first."

She rolled over, pushed up on her knees, putting her round ass in front of him. Darnell smiled. He liked how Starr knew exactly what she wanted and he aimed to please. He took his length and pushed it inside of her; stroking her wetness, making her growl like a lioness in heat. She enjoyed the rough pounding. Never had she had a lover go so deep. She enjoyed every inch he gave her. Darnell, on the other hand, was enjoying how flexible she was as he bent her in one position after another. Soon he put her on her back and gave her one endless stroke after another. In the midst of their love making the unexpected occurred.

"I love you," he whispered.

Starr paused and stared at him. He never said that to her before. She knew what she felt for him was intense but didn't want to be the first to say it. For him to say it just confirmed the feelings were mutual. Still feeling him deep between her legs she replied, "I love you too."

He smiled, kissed her, and they continued to make love to each other until the break of dawn.

MY CURRENT SITUATION   BY   MARLON MCCAULSKY

Crush On You

All through his life Jason, for the most, part got by on his charm and good looks. He realized at the tender age of nine that girls thought he was cute and they chased him. Armed with that knowledge he became a master in the game of women. He was almost never without a female in his life and very rarely let his feelings get caught up. Jason always stayed in a playa frame of mind but even a playa can be taken by surprise.

He sat on the couch after work flipping through channels on TV not able to find what he wanted to watch. He looked at his phone and checked the messages. He was looking for anything from Deja. She had always sent him a text asking him to come through but for the past week he hadn't heard from her. He knew she was a bit pissed at him for popping up over her house the other night but knew after the way he put it on her she was more than satisfied. Hell, he impressed himself, so that's why he was confused why she hadn't text him saying how good it was like she usually did. He thought about texting her but decided to call her instead.

After a few rings Deja answered. "Hello?"

"Hey, what's up?"

"Nothing."

"I haven't heard from you in a while."

"I've been busy with work."

"Oh." A brief moment of dead silence went by. Deja was not her normal talkative self he noticed. "So what are you doing tonight, ma?"

"Nothing really."

"Mind if I come through?"

Deja sighed. "Actually, I think I'm gonna turn in early and get some rest. I'm not in the mood for company."

Jason sulked but didn't want to sound too

120

disappointed by her decision. "Oh okay. Well you know I need you to be completely rested and ready when I come over. You know how I do!"

"Yeah okay. I'ma go lay down now, Jay." Deja was unresponsive to his cockiness.

"Aight. I'll talk to you later." He heard the line disconnect.

He pulled the phone away from his ear and looked at it. Jason was completely baffled at Deja's lack of interest in talking to him. He suddenly felt a feeling he hadn't felt in years—rejection. He hasn't felt that since Selena. The one woman he truly loved just burned out on him with no explanation. Jason quickly pushed those memories of Selena out of his head. He really wanted to see Deja and get some more of her good loving but instead, he sat back on the couch and channel surfed for something to take his mind off of Selena.

~~~

ATLANTA - DEJA'S APARTMENT

Across town, Deja ended her phone call with Jason and looked her reflection in the full length mirror admiring how good she looked in her teal hued dress that accented all of her sexy curves. She was dressed to go out with Kurt for their first date and was excited. She didn't mind blowing Jason off. The more she thought about it the more she realized that she was just using him to catch a nut. What she was beginning to feel was something she hadn't felt in years—butterflies. She was not going to miss this date tonight for anything.

Once she was done making sure her hair was on point she picked up her clutch and walked to the living room.

Just then, the doorbell rang and she felt a rush of excitement run through her. She quickly went to the door, opened it and saw Kurt standing in front of her looking like

GQ model. He wore a white button down, with black jeans, and white sneakers. This brother sure knew how to put himself together she thought.

"Hey, wow!" He cuffed his hand over his mouth admiring Deja in her dress. "You look great."

She blushed. "If you say so. You looking pretty clean too."

"Just a little sumpin' I pulled out the closet," he mused. "You ready to go?"

She smiled. "Yes."

Kurt drove to Kat's Cafe on Piedmont Avenue. It was a small nightclub with signature martinis known for live music. Tonight on stage was an Atlanta native, Eva Kennedy, a Rock and Soul artist with an incredible voice and an electrifying stage performance. Once inside they got a table and ordered their drinks and meal. Kurt couldn't help but smile at how stunning Deja looked tonight. She could feel his eyes on her.

"You're staring at me."

"I know," he replied. "You look beautiful."

Deja blushed. "Ah, thank you."

"Why do you seem surprised to hear me say that?"

"I'm just not used to guys saying that to me."

"Yeah right. I'm sure you get plenty of compliments."

"No, honestly I don't. I get guys saying, 'Damn shawty you thick, 'Girl you fine', 'You tryna' fuck tonight', and stuff like that. I'm not used to guys saying I'm beautiful."

Kurt gazed in her eyes. "Well you should, because you are."

Deja couldn't fight the smile that spread across her face hearing him say that to her. Most men would only spit game to her and say whatever to get some ass. But Kurt was really taking her off guard.

"Can I ask you something?" Deja inquired.

"Anything."

"What the hell do you really do for a living?"

"What do you mean?" He laughed. "You know I what I do."

"I'm starting to think your real name is Tommy."

"Oh you got jokes!" He looked at her perplexed. "Really, after all these years, you don't know?"

"Kinda sorta but not really," she told him honestly. "Yes I know you own a recording studio but I've never been clear to what you actually do."

"I can't believe you. All these years?" He shook his head. "I produce music!"

"You know, that's what I thought but I didn't want to just assume! But then sometimes Starr mentions someone is shooting a movie at your studio so I was a little confused."

The waitress returned with their drinks. Kurt sipped his Coke and Rum. "We rent the studio out to up and coming filmmakers. That's something I'm thinking about dabbling in too. I like getting behind the camera."

"Look at you Mr. Producer Director! I knew you were talented but I had no idea."

"Well now you know." He glanced at the stage. "I'm dying to get Eva Kennedy in my studio to record some music. She got that kind of voice that just moves your soul."

"Yes she does." She smiled. "I bet you be getting all kind of groupies up there too. Doing anything to be a star, calling your name, *Mr. Bishop I'll do anything to be put on!*"

He half chuckled. "It's not like that, but yeah, I have had few young ladies try do the most for some studio time."

"Is that what they call it?" She chuckled. "I bet you like it when girls call your name."

Kurt smiled. "No, I'm not into little girls. I like grown women, like you."

Deja exhaled and took a gulp of her drink.

After they ate dinner neither one was ready for the night to end so they got up and danced to the music being played in the café; H.E.R. *"Every Kind Of Way"*.

They danced face-to-face, their bodies pressing tightly

against one another.

♪*I wanna please you, no matter how long it takes*

Their lips were inches away from each other. After years of friendship neither knew the chemistry that brewed just beneath the surface as they looked into each other's eyes.

♪*If the world should end tomorrow, then we only have today*

Deja brushed her lips against Kurt's and he pulled her in.

♪*I'm gonna love you in every kind of way*

They danced and kissed moving their bodies to the intoxicating rhythm of the song. It was without a doubt the best kiss either of them ever had in their life.

Soon enough it was closing time and Kurt drove Deja back to her apartment. Even though they had been out for almost three hours it felt like the night had only begun. Once he pulled into her apartment complex Kurt got out, opened the passenger door and walked Deja to her apartment still engaged in conversation. A part of her wanted to invite him in but she was nervous of what he would think of her. This was different than when she hooked up with Jason. He only wanted sex from her and that's all she wanted as well. But with Kurt she felt something a little bit deeper. She felt a rush of nerves as she fiddled for her keys inside of her clutch. Kurt could feel her nervousness. She unlocked her door and turned to face him.

"So when can I see you again," he asked.

Deja smiled. "Whenever you want to. I would invite you in but—"

"Deja." Kurt stopped her. "I didn't take you out to sleep with you. I wanted to have a good time with you and I did. Trust me, when the time is right, you'll know it."

He leaned in and gave her a kiss. Once again she felt butterflies flutter inside of her.

He pulled away. "Goodnight."

"Night." She waved and went inside.

Unbeknownst to them, Jason was parked in the back

of the parking lot. He went over to her place in the hopes of getting some late night action like he did last time. He figured she'd be good and rested by now. To his surprise he saw her getting out of Kurt's car. He couldn't believe it, she lied and told him she was staying in but went out instead.

He watched him walking back to his car. "Kurt?"

He was confused. When did this happen? He knew they were friends but he always figured Kurt was chasing Danielle. He watched him pull out of the parking lot. Even though Deja wasn't his lady he still felt some kind of way inside seeing her with another man. If Kurt thought he could swoop in on his thing then he had another thing coming.

Why First Dates Shouldn't Be Embarrassing

DECATUR - DANIELLE'S CONDO

Danielle was sprawled across her bed resting. She spent the day at the hospital with Ms. Sharon, and of course, she saw Rick. It was awkward. They really didn't say much to one another but his eyes said it all. Every now and then she would catch his gaze and for a second she would feel something she thought wasn't there anymore. Her cell phone began to ring and she looked at the display. Her mood lightened seeing Ken Hayes on the display.

"Hello?"

"Hello Dani. Did I catch you at a bad time?"

"No," she told him, relieved. "I was just wondering if you were gonna call me or not."

"Well you know I had to give you the standard two day waiting period before I did."

"If you say so. Are you done running the background check on me?"

"Yes," he chortled, "and I have good news."

"What's that?"

"You came back clean and now I can take you out in public."

"Whatever," Danielle dismissed. "Assuming your background check comes back clean mister, where did you want to take me?"

"I was thinking we could go to the zoo or something and then maybe get a bite to eat?"

"When?"

"Assuming I don't have any priors, how about tomorrow say about eleven?"

Danielle smiled. "Of course. I'll text you tomorrow Mr. Hayes."

~~~

Danielle questioned her decision to go out today with Ken. Not that he was a bad guy because he really seemed like a good man. Her doubts rested within herself. Was she ready to start something new? She had half a mind to call Ken and cancel right now but part of her missed being with a man. She wasn't ready to become a hermit yet.

It was a few minutes before he was due to arrive and Danielle was dressed and ready to go with Ken to the Zoo. She wore dark blue jeans, a yellow blouse with a black tank top underneath, and black and white Vans. Her hair was pulled back into a ponytail allowing her bang to fall slightly over her right eye. Just as she was putting the finishing touches on her hair, the doorbell rang. She headed downstairs, took a deep breath then opened the door.

"Hey there," Ken greeted with a smile.

Danielle blushed. "Hey you!"

Ken looked nice, dressed in a dark green button shirt with the selves rolled up and blue jeans. Danielle laughed to herself seeing him and thought maybe he and Kurt shopped at the same stores. Ken, once again, was awestruck. He was really feeling her vibe and was determined to get to know her better.

"You ready to see the monkeys?" He jokingly asked.

"I sure am."

"Then let's do it."

Danielle closed her front door and followed him to his car. After a brief drive through the city they arrived at the Atlanta Zoo. They walked around the park looking at the animals. It was a little awkward at first. She hadn't gone on many dates over the years. Most of the men she dated were lawyers like her. The conversation would often be work related but with Ken she didn't have that common ground. He could feel her uneasiness and decided to make her laugh with his jokes about the animals.

The good news he was easy on the eyes and Danielle enjoyed looking at his handsome face. Soon, she found herself having a good time. After an hour of walking around they decided to grab some lunch at one of the park's food stands. Ken got two hotdogs and fries while Danielle got a funnel cake and a Sprite.

"Are you enjoying yourself?" He popped a few fries in his mouth.

Danielle picked at the funnel cake. She knew he would ask something of the sort. She put a small piece in her mouth and wanted to devour the whole thing. Instead, she pursed her lips then drank some of her soda. "Yes, I am. Why do you ask?"

"I could tell by the way you were looking that you didn't seem comfortable."

She knew he could sense her uneasiness no matter how well she tried to play it off. "I wasn't feeling well," she lied.

"Why didn't you tell me?" He had a genuinely concerned look on his face. "We could've gone out some other time."

"It kinda came on all of a sudden and I didn't want to disappoint you," she explained. "I feel better now."

Ken smiled. "I think there's very little you can do that would really disappoint me."

Danielle thought to herself how many times she has heard other men say something like that until the real them surfaced. They were a cheater, pervert, on the down low or had about three or four baby mommas stashed away somewhere. She wondered if Ken was like all the other guys and would end up disappointing her in the end.

"Well, I'm having a good time with you," she replied.

"I hope it's the first of many."

Danielle simply smiled and was glad that conversation was over. Now she could eat her dessert like she wanted. While Ken really seemed like a great guy at this present juncture, she wasn't going to get her hopes up thinking this could turn into something. She made that mistake before and was not going end up with a broken heart again.

They continued to enjoy their time at the Zoo. She looked at her phone and saw it was 5:57pm. Ken glanced over at her and was glad he decided to ask her out. He wasn't ready for the day to end.

"Would you like to go to Uptown with me tonight?"

Danielle looked at him. It's not like she had something else to do at home. Besides Ken was fun to be around. Why not spend some more time with him.

"Sure."

The two left the Zoo and headed to the Uptown Comedy club on Marietta Street. Once they went inside they had a seat at a little table in the middle of the club. The waitress stopped at their table.

"Hi, my name is Tiffany. I'll be serving you tonight. What can I get for you?"

"Just water please," Danielle replied.

The waitress turned to Ken. "And for you?"

"I'll have a Rum and Coke."

"Great! I'll be right back out with your drinks."

She moved on to her next table and Ken looked at Danielle. "You know it's okay if you want to get something stronger than water. It won't break me," he joked.

"I'm good, I don't need anything else," Danielle responded, colder than she intended. Ken nodded his head and Danielle could feel the awkwardness he felt. Truth was, she and Rick used to frequent the club and couldn't help but think of him every time she looked at Ken.

"So when was the last time you went out to a comedy show," he asked.

"It's been awhile," she replied, honestly.

129

"Oh, well I heard this dude Bobby Redd is pretty funny."

"Yeah, okay."

Ken could see his attempts to make small talk were failing. He couldn't understand the change in demeanor and wondered if she just wasn't feeling him. The waitress returned with their drinks and Danielle could tell that he was trying the best to connect with her. She felt like a jerk. Why couldn't she just let go and enjoy herself with him?

"Excuse me for a minute."

"Okay." He nodded.

Danielle got up and went to the ladies room. It was empty. She went to the mirror and stared at her reflection. *Get it together Dani. You got a handsome man dying to make you enjoy yourself. So stop fucking it up,* she thought. A few minutes later she returned to their table and smiled at Ken.

"You won't believe what happened to me in there." She shook her head feigning disgust.

Ken had a look of concern on his face. "What?"

"I was just in the ladies room and there was some chick in the other stall blowing up the joint!"

"Oh hell nah!" Ken laughed. "She was just letting it go like that?"

"All up in there breaking bad!"

"I didn't think y'all did that kind of stuff in public."

"Are you kidding me?" Danielle laughed. "You would be shocked how disgusting some of these cute looking chicks are in public restrooms. All kinds of things be up in there!"

He leaned in closer, very curious. "Like what?"

"I've seen used tampons, panties in the bowl, even condoms. I mean some these hoes out here are just doing the most!" She shook her head.

Ken cracked up with laughter.

"But I don't understand what's so hard about flushing the damn toilet. I don't wanna see or smell that shit! I swear some of these chicks be taking dumps like they're a truck driver!"

"Oh my god!" He gazed at her. "So have you ever…"

She frowned. "Ever what?"

"You know, taken a deuce in public?"

She gawked. "Hell no!"

"C'mon Dani, not once in your life have you released the beast in public?"

"Nope." She protested. "I will hold that shit in till I get my ass home!"

With a big smile on his face. "Really? You never once been caught out there?"

"Listen, I can't believe I'm going to tell you this, on our first date and all but I make a habit of doing the doo every morning before I leave the house. If I have to go at work, I have my own private bathroom so there's no getting caught out there. So do you poop in public Mr. Hayes?"

He looked at her for a second. "Yes I do."

She scrounged her nose. "Ewwww! Oh my god! You nasty!"

"There is nothing wrong with pooping in public."

"Oh really?"

"Of course not! Bowel movements are something we literally all have, or should be having on a regular basis. Hey, you hold that shit in for too long you'll mess around and kill yourself!"

"Whatever!"

"Hey, I work in the medical field I've seen some shit." They both laughed. "All I'm saying is I ain't dying because I refuse to use a public bathroom."

"Well you just make sure when you're out on a date with me your bowels are empty!"

"Well I guess we know which one of us is full of shit." He grinned.

Danielle laughed and gently smacked his arm. "Shut up! You're not funny!"

They both laughed and exchanged glances. Danielle's

little lie broke the ice between them. She knew she had to lighten the mood and what better way was to talk about poop.

Soon the show began and the first comedian took the stage and the crowd responded well to her jokes. Danielle found herself laughing along with Ken at her antics. Ken looked and saw a smile on Danielle's face and knew this was a good idea.

After the female comedian was done, two more comedians donned the stage, then the headliner, Bobby Redd. Immediately, Danielle began laughing at his jokes. He was funnier than Ken mentioned. They both lost it when Bobby joked about an ex-girlfriend who used to leave her shitty panties around the bedroom and how nasty she was. They were literally crying by the end of his set.

After the show the two went to Ihop for breakfast. Danielle had the blueberry pancakes while Ken ordered a big steak omelet. Although their day started off shaky; by the end of the night, they really opened up to each other and Rick was the furthest thing from her mind.

After dinner Ken drove her home. Once they arrived he walked her to the front door. Danielle thought even though they started enjoying each other's company in the end, most the date was a disaster and it was her fault. She was sure he wouldn't want to waste any more time with her. She unlocked her front door.

"So Dani, when can we get together again?"

"You want to go out with me again?"

"Yeah, I do."

She was shocked. Either he really liked her or was desperate for company because she wouldn't want to go out with her again if she was him.

She thought about it for a second and smiled. "I'd like that."

Ken leaned in and kissed her softly. She enjoyed the feel of his lips against hers and made her feel some type of way inside.

He slowly pulled away. "Goodnight Dani."

"Goodnight."

.

Sex Ain't Better Than Love

Deja was feeling good today. As a matter of fact she had been feeling good all week because of her growing relationship with Kurt. In all the years she had known him she never really thought this would ever happen mainly because she knew he had a thing for Danielle. Over the last few weeks Deja had taken a very honest look at her life and wasn't too proud of a lot of her decisions.

Deja sat on the couch reading text messages that she had been exchanging with Kurt all week. Most of them were playful and flirtatious about their date. Deja was surprised when he told her he had been thinking of her for a while but didn't want to step to her because he wasn't sure how she saw him. Yet another misjudgment in men she thought.

Deja got a few texts from Jason wanting to hook up again. She continued to give him one excuse after another about her being busy. She liked him as a friend but she was more interested where things were going with Kurt.

Today he told her he was going to take her somewhere special for lunch but wouldn't say where. She received a text from him letting her know he was almost at her place. She decided to meet him in the parking lot. It was an unusually warm day as the sun shined brightly in the sky. Two minutes later Kurt pulled up and Deja couldn't help but smile. She was really starting to fall for this man.

He stepped out of his car. "I see you looking good as usual."

"Thank you." She blushed. She wanted to kiss him but gave him a hug instead. She didn't want to seem too sprung. Kurt held her body tight and inhaled the sweet fragrance on her neck. He instantly felt himself becoming aroused so he gently pulled away trying to control himself.

"So, you ready to go?"

"Yeah, where we going again?"

He walked her to the passenger side of his car and opened the door. "Nice try, but you'll find out when we get there."

"C'mon just give me a hint," she begged.

Kurt smiled at her. "Hmmmm … Nah!"

He closed her door, went around to the driver side and got in.

Deja folded her arms across her chest and playfully pouted. "You are so mean to me."

"We'll see what you say when we get there," he told her.

Deja smiled and leaned back in the seat as Kurt pulled off. After a few minutes of driving she soon realized where he was taking her. "Lake Lanier? What are we gonna do there?"

Kurt glanced at her. "You'll see."

They pulled up in front in front of the landmark and parked. The view of the lake was serene as the sunlight sparkled in its blue waters. Kurt popped the trunk and got out of the car. Deja wondered what was he doing and was pleasantly surprised to see him return to the driver side with a picnic basket.

"When was the last time a man took you on a picnic?"

Deja laughed. "Okay … you got me, never! I hope you got something good in there."

Kurt's brow crinkled. "I only do the best."

They got out of the car, walked to a nearby picnic table, and had a seat. He opened the basket and showed her four corned beef sandwiches wrapped individually in Ziploc bags. Another Ziploc with sweet kernel popcorn and four cans of peach Crush soda.

Deja giggled. "Now you know I love corned beef sandwiches! And where did you find peach Crush in a can? Every time I go to the super market I can't find them."

He picked up a sandwich and handed it to her.

"Cause you ain't looking at the right place. I got these at the BP gas station on Flat Shoals Road. Near the I85 North entrance ramp," he revealed.

"Oh! I'm gonna go there and get me a twelve pack!" Deja declared. "This is so … nice Kurt. I've never had anyone do something like this for me."

He smiled. "Well I'm happy to be the first." He opened the soda can and handed it to her then opened one for himself and held it up to toast. "Here's to new beginnings."

Deja tapped her can against his. "To new beginnings."

They spent the next hour enjoying each other's company. They walked around the lake then sat on a bench enjoying its splendor. Deja couldn't believe what a good time she was having.

She looked at Kurt. "Not too many men would even think of doing something like this ya'know?"

"Thought you knew by now, I'm not like most men."

"I know, you're special."

Kurt put his arm around her and held her close. Everything felt right. Another hour passed and Kurt drove Deja back home. Once there he walked her to her front door and she opened it.

"Would you like to come inside?"

"Absolutely."

He followed her inside and she closed the door behind her. Deja felt butterflies fluttering in her stomach. She never felt this way with any other man but having Kurt there made her feel excited, nervous, and horny all at the same time.

"So this is my fabulous apartment." She turned to face him and nervously pulled her hair back behind her ear. "Bet you didn't know I was an interior decorator on the side huh," she joked, gesturing her hands around.

Kurt maintained his focus on Deja's face. "Gorgeous," he replied not talking about her apartment.

Deja blushed. "Can I get you a drink or something? I'm sure I got some wine in the fridge."

She attempted to walk by Kurt to get to the kitchen but he took her hand. "I got what I need right here."

He pulled her close and kissed her. Deja melted in his arms. His hands caressed her soft ass in her jeans and Deja could feel the hardness growing in his. This time Kurt didn't mind her feeling it and neither did she. As a matter of fact since the night of their first kiss Deja had been curious about what he was working with. Everything about him had been almost too good to be true she thought.

She pulled away and led him to her bedroom a few feet away. She turned around and faced him and Kurt moved closer. She unzipped her fly and Kurt slid his hand inside of her jeans. He looked into her eyes as if asking permission to go further. Her smile was his signal to continue and he pulled her jeans down mid-thigh admiring her in her pink panties. Deja sat down on the bed and peeled her jeans off. Kurt got what she assumed was a condom from his pocket and began to undress slowly, teasing her. Just then, Deja realized she was eye level with his crotch. Was he gonna want some head right off the bat she thought? Not that she against giving it but it wasn't the first thing she wanted to do with him. Once she saw what he was working with after he eased his boxers down Deja was astonished by the size of the penis in front of her. Her eyes went up to his face then back down to his hard shaft. This man was truly blessed she thought.

He laid her back on the bed and continued his pursuit of her. She was glad he wasn't interested in getting some head as he kissed her lips. Kurt pulled Deja's panties off and tossed them next to her bra on the floor. His right hand caressed her breasts, trailed down her body and rested between her thighs.

"I've wanted you for so long," he whispered, rubbing her heat causing her to moan softly.

"You don't have to say that," she replied, having heard the same words before.

"I don't say what I don't mean." He replaced his fingers on her clit with the tip of his manhood and stirred her wetness. Only pushing the tip inside he rubbed up and down her moist pink slit. She touched his hardness still amazed with his length and girth.

He kissed her lips. "You like that?"

"Yes," she hummed.

Kurt eased up off of her and opened the condom in his left hand, rolled it on, then slowly pushed his penis inside of her inch by inch.

Kurt watched as Deja's face contorted feeling him slide deeper inside of her. With her legs spread wide he stroked her moist well slow and deep making sure she felt every inch he was giving her. Kurt bit his bottom lip and closed his eyes as her heat surrounded him. She felt better than he imagined. He kissed her neck and whispered sweet nothings in her ear while Deja moaned and mumbled something inaudible as if she was begging for mercy. Kurt; however, wasn't interested in showing any mercy and sped up his long deep stroke; swaying his hips back and forth like a seesaw making Deja moan as he hit the bottom of her of her love. Kurt felt her vagina clinch his penis and cum as he continued his work.

"Oh, shit," Deja moaned. "Don't stop!"

"I don't plan to," Kurt confirmed.

They spent the next few hours making love in almost every position they could imagine and a few they just came up with by accident. Kurt went above and beyond Deja's expectations in pleasing her. He made her feel things so intense that there were no words for her to describe it. He wasn't just trying to beat it up he was making her feel like a woman. Deja realized that this was more than just great sex this was what it felt like when a man made love to a woman. When they finally ran out of strength Deja rested her head on his chest.

"Why did it take so long for this to happen," she asked.

"It happened when it was supposed to," he affirmed. "How was it?"

"It was aight. She paused for a second but couldn't contain herself. "I can't even front. You were the shit."

They both laughed.

"You too." Kurt exhaled. "Whew…"

Deja shook her head. "I can't believe I'm here with you like this. I never saw this coming."

"Do you wanna continue to be with me like this?"

She looked into his eyes. "Yes, I do. I want to see where this goes."

"Good, because I do too. What about, you know, everybody else?"

"I'm not trying to hide what we have but I don't wanna announce it to everybody yet. I really like being with you and I don't want folks in our business," she explained. "I know what some people think about me. I don't always make the best decisions."

"It doesn't matter what anybody thinks about you. As long as you're honest with me, I'll be honest with you. That's all that matters."

She smiled. "I glad you can see the real me."

"I always did. This is the start of something special and I wanna protect that. So whatever you want to do is fine with me."

GAME TIME!

DECATUR - JASON'S HOUSE

Kurt was on his way to Jason's to watch the Hawks versus Cavs playoff game. They were more acquaintances than friends; Mike was the mutual connection they shared but they were always cool. The three men would hang out occasionally and watch games. He was a regular at Jason's Lounge along with Mike, Kima, and Danielle. The Atlanta Hawks making the playoffs was a rare event so coming together to watch them play the Cavs was something he looked forward to. Kurt knocked on Jason's door and a few moments went by before it opened.

"Wus up," Mike greeted, giving him a shoulder hug.

Kurt walked inside. "I'm chillin' man."

He saw Jason on the couch with a paper plate full of wings on his lap.

"What's up Jay?" Kurt gave him some dap.

"Same ol' shit, bruh," Jason retorted.

"The game start yet?"

"They about to tip off now," he replied. "Yo, I got some wings on the table and some beer in the fridge. Go help yo self."

"That's what's up!" Kurt walked toward the kitchen. "Oh shit, you got Teriyaki too? I'ma go in!"

Mike sat back down on the couch with Jason and took his Heineken to the head. Jason watched Kurt fix himself a plate. He was still a bit annoyed that he was the reason Deja had been blowing him off and that wasn't sitting well with him. Sure, it was only sex between them, but the look he saw on her face with Kurt was pure delight ... something he never saw. *That fool must be getting all romantic and*

140

shit with her. Ain't no way he putting it on her better than me, he thought to himself. At any rate he was gonna have a laugh or two at Kurt's expense tonight.

He returned with a plate of wings and had a seat on the other couch.

"You straight, Kurt?" Jason asked.

He picked up a wing. "Hell yeah, I'm good now!"

Jason smiled knowing that he wouldn't be 'good' by the time the game was over. The game started and they watched the Hawks take an early six point lead over the Cavs. It looked like the Hawks were hyped as hell as they ran the court. A few more minutes went by before they heard another knock on the door. Jason smiled knowing who it was. He got up off the couch and walked down the hallway to answer the door. Both Mike and Kurt kept their attention on the game that was now tied.

Jason returned. "Hey ah… guess who decided to come though."

In walked Rick and Darnell. Both Kurt and Mike frowned at their arrival. Mike was less than thrilled to see the man who he had a strong suspicion of messing with his sister. He had been meaning to ask Jason about him but since he was there he could find out about him first hand.

"Yo, what's up fellas?" Rick made eye contact with everybody.

"What's up?" Darnell greeted.

Mike got up and gave Rick a shoulder hug but only shot Darnell a quick head nod.

Truth was even though Rick's relationship with Danielle ended badly he was still cool with everybody else except Kurt.

Kurt; however, stayed seated with a screw face painted on.

Last time the two saw each other was when his fist connected with Rick's jaw sending him down to the ground in front of their friends.

Jason watched closely. If it was time for Rick to get payback, now was the time and he knew it.

"What's up, Kurt?" Rick glared at him which caused Kurt to dart up, ready for war.

Darnell sat down totally unaware of the beef.

Mike, seeing the look on Kurt's face, knew it was about to get ugly.

"Everybody just take it easy." His burly body stood between the two men.

"What the hell is he doing here, Jay?" Kurt asked.

Jason shrugged his shoulders. "I didn't think it'll be a problem. You didn't know Rick was back in town? My bad!"

"Yeah I knew." He glared at Jason like he was stupid. "But you didn't say he was coming here tonight."

"Listen Kurt," Rick spoke up. "I didn't come here tonight to fight." Kurt look angrily at him not letting his guard down. He was ready to pop off. "Seriously, bruh."

"Aight what you here for?" Kurt asked boldly.

Rick took a deep breath. "I needed to get away from the hospital for a while. And I wanna apologize to you."

Kurt looked at him confused. "Apologize?"

Rick nodded. "Yeah listen, I was out of line that night. I let my insecurities get the best of me and because of that ... I hurt Danielle and truly regret it."

Kurt nodded. "Okay, so now what? You apologized and now you think it's cool to go after her again?"

Rick sighed. "Nah bruh, that ship done sailed. Danielle hates my guts. I'm the last person she wants back in her life and I understand. I fucked up."

"Yeah, you did," Kurt confirmed.

"Bruh, I just want you to know, I ain't got no beef with you. I'm responsible for what happened that night and I'm sorry." Rick extended his hand.

He hesitated momentarily before he shook it. As much as he didn't like him he had to respect the fact that he manned up and apologized. Mike breathed a sigh of relief while Jason rolled his eyes hoping Rick would've went ham on him.

"I'm sorry to hear about your mom," Kurt said sincerely. "She's like all of our moms."

Rick nodded. "Thanks man."

"Well now that's out the way," Mike chimed in, "can we watch the game?"

Both Kurt and Rick chuckled. "We good."

The atmosphere lightened and Rick had a seat on the lounger behind him. "Who's winning?"

"The Heat," Mike replied.

The camaraderie between all of the men became better but Jason still sat brooding. Kurt and Rick made idle conversation about the game easing the tension that was there before. Surprisingly to both men they realized they agreed a lot on the analyses of each team. Jason still wanted to get under Kurt's skin and knew the best way to do it.

"So Kurt, I haven't seen you around that much. You got a new chick stashed away somewhere?"

Kurt didn't want to tell them that he was seeing Deja. Knowing her rather explicit history was bad enough he didn't want to be reminded of it. "Yeah, I got a sweet girl around the way I'm seeing."

"Sweet," Jason repeated. "Uh oh, you done found yourself a little tender roni, huh?"

"Yeah, she's a good girl."

"They be the freakiest ones man. You must be tearing that ass up."

Kurt simply nodded not wanting to talk about his sex life. Since the first night they made love it had been on ever since. He knew they had something special.

"Well that's great you found a good one, bruh," Rick confirmed. "If she's the right one don't let her get away."

"Oh trust me, I know. And he might be, she might be."

Jason was annoyed by his words and decided to revise

his attack. "Yo Mike, how's married life?"

"We good, she's moody as hell but you know how women are," he quipped. "I knew how she was from the day we met."

"Yeah, I know. I get that same attitude from Deja." He shook his head.

Kurt glared at him. What did Jason mean by that he wondered? He knew they were friends but never more than that.

Jason could tell by the look on Kurt's face he had hit a nerve. He continued. "You would think after I done smashed that ass she would be in a good mood, right?"

Mike did a double take. "Wait a minute? You and Deja have been hooking up?"

"Yeah man, I been hitting that on the regular for a while now. I'm just saying, you know what I mean tho, right? When you put it on that ass they start acting like they got some damn sense. Deja is a stone cold freak. She be feenin' for it."

Kurt sat back on the couch looking at the TV trying to control his emotions but he was brewing inside.

Jason looked at Rick. "You know she came up to the club one time and broke me off in the back room. I damn near had to beg her to stop." He smiled at the memory.

Kurt was getting more pissed by the second. He never knew about them.

"You wilding out, Jay." Rick drank more of his beer.

"Dude, I know you were all booed up with Dani but you can't tell me you ain't think about hitting Deja's ass at least once."

Rick snickered. "Of course. Truthfully, all of them are fine as hell. Deja, Dani and Starr."

"Hey hey hey!" Mike interjected taken off guard.

"No offense, man. I know she's your sister."

"I know, and actually, it's not y'all I don't trust." He affixed his glare at Darnell who shifted in his seat.

"My point is any man would get with them," Rick explained.

"You right about that. Between the three of us we done hit nearly all of them. Starr would be on my radar but I think she might be off the market now," Jason joked and looked at Mike.

Mike gave him the side eye and made a fist. "You play too much."

"I'm just fucking wit you man! But whoever's with her must be having the time of his life." Jason purposely threw that out there and Darnell cringed. He could feel Mike burning a hole through him.

"But now that I think about it, Rick, you need to go ahead and smash Deja. Keep it in the family bruh." He laughed.

Kurt was at his boiling point and wanted to punch Jason dead in the face. Why was he talking about Deja so much he wondered? They always talked about women amongst them but he was being extra tonight.

Rick shook his head. "Wow, you on one tonight, Jay."

"Trust me dawg, I got some ass from her just two weeks ago and that shit was nice and tight. She looked like she was getting ready to go somewhere but I had to cancel those plans. That girl know she can take some dick!"

Kurt had heard enough. If he didn't leave now he was going kick Jason's ass in his house.

He got up. "Yo, I gotta go take care of some business. I'll holla at y'all later."

He left without giving anybody any dap. Jason reveled with satisfaction seeing the frustration on Kurt face. The front door slammed shut. Mike, Rick, and Darnell looked at Jason.

"What the hell was that about?" Rick asked.

He knew Jason better than most. There was something going on that nobody was in on.

Jason shrugged his shoulders. "Karma baby."

"Speaking of which, Darnell, you got something you wanna tell me?" Mike glared at him.

Darnell nodded. "I guess it's not a secret any more huh? Your sister and I have been seeing each other."

"Nice of one of you to tell me."

"Don't blame her, it was me," he lied. "I just wanted us to get to know each other before we let the world know."

"Really?" Mike leaned forward. "So how well does my sister know you?"

"Well enough," Darnell told him matter-of-factly. "Listen Mike, Starr is a very smart woman. She's very different from the other women I've dated."

"Other women? How many others are there?" Mike looked at Jason who shook his head and finished his beer. "I know how you get down. So Darnell, are you a ho like Jason?"

"Why I gotta be a ho?" Jason interjected.

Mike ignored his question. "So if you're anything like him, should I be worried about what your plans are for my sister?"

"Trust me, the only plans I have for your sister is to treat her right."

Mike glared at Darnell then got up from his seat. "I gotta go take a piss."

He walked down the hallway to the bathroom. Jason was cracking up.

Darnell looked at him. "You really got no chill tonight, huh?"

"Relax! He ain't gonna do nothing. Trust me!"

Kill – Screw - Marry

Since the fellas all decided to get together at Jason's place for the Hawks playoff game Kima decided to invite the ladies over for movie night. Which, in most cases, became a drinking and shit talking. She was in the kitchen getting the drinks ready while the girls were in the living room sitting in front of the TV.

Starr popped in the *No Good Deed* DVD and Deja licked her lips. "Idris could invade my home anytime."

"That man know he's fine," Starr added.

Danielle looked at her. "Better be careful, your brother might have the place bugged."

"I know right." She exhaled. "Next thing you know Mike would be on the next plane to London looking to fight Idris."

Danielle chuckled. "He ain't all that anyway."

"What?" Deja glared at her sister like she had two heads. "I thought you of all people would jump on his fine ass!"

"He's just a man."

Kima entered the room with drinks on a tray. "Who's just a man?"

Starr took a glass of Moscoto. "Idris."

"Ooohh yeah, that fine tall dark chocolate man, yummy," Kima sang as Deja reached for a Corona.

She took a sip and chimed in. "Dani said he ain't all that."

"Really," Kima questioned.

Danielle took a Corona as well. "C'mon, you take away his muscles, flawless chocolate skin, English accent, and what do you got?"

Deja looked at her. "Rick."

"You ain't funny." Danielle gave her sister the middle

148

finger.

"Okay," Deja looked at Kima. "Would you fuck Idris?"

"Oh yeah, I'd sit on his face."

Starr held up her glass. "I second that motion." Starr held up her glass.

"Objection," Danielle yelled.

"Overruled," Deja barked. "Girl, court has spoken. Idris could get it!"

"Whatever."

Kima stared at her friend. "C'mon Dani, you mean you wouldn't give him the business?"

She rolled her eyes and drank more of her beer. "Yes I would, but it's more to being with a man than sex."

"Well sometimes all you really want is sex from a dude. That's all some of them are really good at," Deja spoke truthfully.

"Well, I look for something a little deeper than just that."

"And sometimes all you need is a man to go deeper!" Starr giggled and so did everybody else.

Danielle looked at her shocked. "What do you know about that?"

"Contrary to what everybody might think; despite my brother's interferences, I have a great sex life."

Kima looked at her. "With who?"

All eyes turned toward her waiting for an answer. She put the wine glass up to her lips and downed the golden liquid. "Like you all don't already know who."

"Well, I don't!" Danielle yelled.

"Girl. Starr's been getting that back blown by that fine ass Mr. Darnell Smith," Kima announced.

Danielle's neck craned. "What! Damn Starr, I ain't mad at you! How long has this been going on?"

"A couple of months now. I've never been with a man so, blessed!" She bragged. "The way he makes me feel is just …" Starr shivered and blushed.

"So damn, he be putting down like that?" Deja leaned in toward her friend.

"He be having dick-dick," she said matter of factly.

"Dick-dick?"

"You know, when he nut and still be hard as fuck!"

They all busted out laughing.

"But you all have got to keep Mike out of my business. Y'all know how annoying he can be."

Kima nodded. "Don't worry he won't hear anything from us."

"Okay, so let's play a game!" Deja suggested.

"What kind of game?" Danielle looked at her sister knowing how her mind worked.

"Kill Fuck Marry." Deja looked at all of them and smiled slyly.

"Oh Lord," Danielle sighed and shook her head. "Why must we?"

"Stop being such a punk, Dani." Kima knocked back her glass of rum and Coke. "It's just a game. What are you scared of?"

Danielle glared at Kima. She didn't like being called out by anybody. She wasn't afraid of any game, especially when she had Corona in her system. She took the bottle to the head and slammed it down on the coffee table.

"Let's get it on!" She looked at Deja. "Who we talking about?"

"Um … let's stick to men we know." Deja winked at her sister.

"Okay. You first."

"We're leaving Mike out of it for obvious reasons." She looked at Kima then back at the girls. "I would fuck Jason, marry Kurt, and kill Rick."

Danielle had a disgusted look on her face. "You would fuck Jason? Are you serious?"

Deja was surprised she didn't say anything about

marrying Kurt. Maybe she didn't feel any type of way about him. She rolled her eyes. "And what? Just because you don't like him doesn't mean he isn't attractive."

"Jason attractive?" She gagged. "I think I just threw up a little in my mouth."

"Stop tripping, Dani. Jason is an attractive man." Kima co-signed.

"I agree," Starr admitted. "He's can be an asshole when he wants to be but he's easy on the eyes."

Danielle shook her head. "I would rather be celibate for the rest of my life than give that cretin some ass."

"When was the last time you got some sis? You seem to be a bit more uptight than usual."

"Don't worry about what I'm getting. I get plenty ... and on the regular!"

Everybody stared at her not believing a word she was saying. Truth was, it had been nearly a year since she had seen any action but she wasn't going to admit that.

Kima snickered. "Better hope you don't give yourself carpal tunnel over there."

"That's not even physically possible!"

"Trust me I've seen stranger things. I can get you a brace if it gets a little rough for you."

Danielle gave her a middle finger. "Well look at that, looks like I still got a full range of motion in my hand. Besides, I got toys for rare occasions smart ass."

"I got batteries too."

Danielle couldn't help but laugh. "I hate you."

"Alrighty then." Deja quipped. "Starr?"

"I would fuck Kurt, marry Darnell," she sang, "and kill Jason."

"Marry Darnell?" Kima looked at her with a raised eyebrow. "Damn girl that dick must be incredible."

Starr gave a smug look. "Well, I ain't one to brag but brother man do know how to swing that wood!"

They all laughed.

"So you really feeling him huh?" Deja asked.

She nodded. "I know we haven't been dating each other for long but yeah I'm really digging him. And yes it's deeper than the sex. I know Darnell can be with almost any woman he wants but he wants me and that's what matters."

Danielle couldn't help but think the last time she felt that way about a man. She was almost jealous that Starr had what she wanted again but she pushed those feelings aside and celebrated along with her.

"That's wonderful, Starr," Danielle told her genuinely. "I hope everything works out for the both of you."

"I think it will. Now, your turn."

Danielle exhaled and all eyes diverted toward her. "Okay, I would kill Jason. Mexican Cartel style." She smiled. "Let's see, I would screw Ken." She paused for moment as she thought about her next choice which everybody was most interested in hearing. She knew what she wanted to say. "I would marry Kurt."

Everyone was quiet as if in shock. Deja was even more surprised. Did she have deeper feelings for Kurt than she had let on? She was going to tell everybody about their relationship but after that, she thought it would be best to keep it to herself.

"Why are you all so quiet?" Danielle asked, looking around.

"No reason." Deja spoke up. "So Ken can get it? I knew you were digging him the other night. I didn't know you were gonna give him the booty this soon."

"Yep. He's nice, fine, and if he got 'dick-dick', I'll let you know," she said boldly.

Deja looked on haphazardly. "I'm scared of you."

"Your turn," Danielle said to Kima.

"Okay, let's say I wasn't married to my husband. I would fuck Kurt. I would kill … Jason. Don't get me wrong I love him like a brother but he can be such a dick at times." She thought for a second. "And I would marry Rick."

Both Starr and Deja were stunned by her last choice. Even though this was just a game she was Danielle's best friend and crossed the unwritten girl's rule. Kima purposely said Rick because she wanted to see how Danielle would react and end up being honest with herself.

She glared at her friend. "Why Rick?"

Kima shrugged her shoulders. "He's a good man. He has a good career, loves his mom, and is attractive."

Danielle took a swig of her beer. "Just didn't think he was your type."

"Tall, dark, and handsome works for me." Kima shrugged her shoulders. "I'm a married woman but there are plenty of single women out there who would snatch him up. It's only a matter of time."

Danielle frowned. "He's flaky and scared of a real woman."

"Maybe? Or maybe he's waiting on the right one."

"Oh please," Danielle retorted. "If Rick hasn't found a woman to put up with his bullshit by now he never will. Besides he wouldn't know what to do if he met a good woman again."

"Why do you still think he's the same person he was six years ago?" Kima asked. "You know people do change. Mature and grow up. I'm pretty sure he's is in a different place than he was back then."

Danielle rolled her eyes. "Well good for him. Where ever that place is he can stay there. I could care less."

There was an uneasy silence.

"Well this game sucked." Deja announced and everyone laughed.

"Well what's going on in your love life," Danielle asked. "You seem to be happy these days."

Deja smiled. "I got a friend."

"Friend got a name?"

"Yeah but I wanna keep it to myself for now. We've known each other for a few years. Funny thing, I never thought a guy like him would be seriously interested in me. I have a feeling he might be the one for me."

Standoffish

THE PARK

For the past three days Deja wondered why Kurt had not responded to any of her calls or texts. At first she thought he was just busy and hadn't had the chance to respond but after the fifth voicemail she left it became clear that he was ignoring her. She began to question what happened. Was it something she had done? They had been enjoying each other company for the last two weeks with no problems and the sex was incredible. *So was he playing me the whole time,* she contemplated but then dismissed that notion. What they had together was real. She knew it so she decided to go to the one place she knew she could find him. She wanted answers and was determined to get them.

As usual, he was on the court with a group of guys playing ball. One of them pointed toward Deja. Kurt turned and saw her standing near her car. She could tell by his body language he wasn't too thrilled to see her. She couldn't for the life of her figure out what she had done. He slowly walked toward her. Shirt off, black basketball shorts on, he was looking good she thought. Kurt stopped a few feet in front of her not making any attempt to hug or kiss her like he usually would.

Deja smiled. "Hey."

"Hey," Kurt replied dryly.

Deja could feel his contempt of her. "Ah ... been calling and texting you for like three days now ... why haven't you hit me back?"

"I've been busy," he retorted.

Deja looked at him confused. "Busy playing basketball?"

"Yeah."

"Why are you treating me like this? What did I do?"

He glared at her. "Why don't you call Jason and ask

him what you did. You seem to have us both on rotation."

Deja was floored. How did he find out about him she wondered?

"Kurt, I haven't seen Jason in weeks and I don't wanna see him."

"Really? When you say weeks you mean two weeks, right?"

She sighed.

He shook his head. "So let me ask you something, the last time you saw him was the same night you were supposed to meet me at Eclipse di Luna for dinner, correct? C'mon lie to me and say it wasn't."

Deja swallowed hard and shook her head trying to hold back her tears. "Kurt, I swear I didn't mean to—"

"You know what," he interrupted. "Forget it. I told you to be honest with me. You should have told me about him from the start. You keep on playing games; I got other things to do."

Kurt turned and trotted back to the basketball court.

Deja couldn't hold back the tears. "Kurt wait, please."

Her plea fell on deaf ears. He began to play ball again as if she weren't there. Deja was devastated. She got in her car and drove away. After dating the wrong type of men for years she finally meets a man who likes her as she is and she messed it up. She had no idea how to fix this or if it could be fixed.

~~~

Rick's mother, in his opinion seemed to be getting stronger; but the truth was, he had a master's degree in Sports Medicine not a degree Cardiology. Her doctor still wanted to keep her for observation. In the meantime Rick settled back in his family home in Decatur. It was a bittersweet homecoming without his mother there. He spent more time at the hospital than at home anyway. Today was no different as he sat in the chair next to his mother's hospital bed.

"How is life in LA, son?"

"Other than the constant sunshine, miles of beaches, and the occasional celebrity scandal? It's bearable."

She smiled. "How do you put up with it?"

They both laughed.

"But in all seriousness mom, I've been considering moving back."

"How come?"

"As great as it is out there, it isn't home. Being here has reminded me how much I miss it. How much I miss you. All of my friends are still here too. It just makes sense."

Sharon wondered if Danielle had anything to do with how he felt.

"What about your job with the Lakers?"

"I've been talking to a few friends with the Hawks and there's a job here if I want it."

She smiled. "It would be nice to have you back home."

"Maybe if I was here with you, I could've—"

"Don't you finish that sentence," his mother said firmly. "Don't you feel any guilt whatsoever about going out and living your life. Your Father would have been proud of you and I am too. You're a good son, Richard."

"And you're an incredible mother." He leaned over and kissed her cheek.

There was a knock on the door and in walked Danielle. It had become sort of a routine for them. Every day at 4pm she would come by. Rick, not wanting to cause any drama, would excuse himself from the room until she left.

"Hello," she greeted and walked toward the bed. "How are we today?"

Sharon smiled. "I'm getting there."

"Well, I'ma get something to eat downstairs. I'll be back." Rick smiled at his mother. Then, as he always did, he looked at Danielle. He wished more than anything that he had a second chance to make things right between them. Once again they made eye contact. Sharon made note of the love she could still see between them.

"I'll be back."

"Okay."

Rick left the room and Danielle took the seat next to Sharon.

"So have the doctors said when they're letting you go home?"

Sharon shrugged. "Maybe on Thursday if my tests come back okay."

"Well that's good! I know you can't wait to sleep in your own bed."

"That would be nice." Sharon looked at Danielle. "Richard said he's going to move back to Atlanta."

She paused. "He did? Oh, well that'll be nice. He can be here for you."

Danielle stood up, poured a cup of water from the pitcher next to Ms. Sharon's bed and gave it to her.

"He said he misses home but I think what he misses the most is you," she spoke frankly.

Danielle sat back down in the chair. "Ms. Sharon, I know you would like to see us get back together but I don't think that's ever going to happen. I've moved on with my life."

"Moved on to what, Danielle? To who? It's been six years and you haven't had a serious relationship since you two broke up. Why is that?"

Danielle was a little lost for words. In all the years she's known Sharon, she's never been so direct. Danielle was a top notch defense attorney and was used to asking tough questions. Being on the receiving end caught her off guard. Sharon had hit her with the truth. She hadn't had a serious relationship that lasted over a year since Rick. She always chalked it up to being too busy with work but what if there was another reason?

"I … I just recently started dating a nice guy."

Sharon smiled. "Well, that sounds wonderful, baby. I hope you listen to your heart because at the end of day, that's what's going to make you really happy."

MY CURRENT SITUATION   BY   MARLON MCCAULSKY

Skew It On The Bar-B

As he did every year, Mike invited everybody to his house for his annual cookout. In a lot of ways he was the glue that kept everybody together over the years. It was so easy for folks to drift apart being caught up in life. This year's cookout would be even better since Rick was in town.

Danielle was looking forward to the event because it would be the first time Ken would meet all of her friends. She wanted to introduce him to everybody but most of all she wanted to show Rick she moved on with her life.

The sun was nice and bright as Danielle and Ken walked hand in hand on the back of Mike's beautifully landscaped lawn. She exhaled deeply when she saw Jason walking toward them with a beer in his hand.

Wus up, Dani?" He gave her a head nod then looked at Ken. "Who dis?"

Danielle shook her head at his rudeness. "This is my friend, Ken," she introduced. "Ken, this ill-mannered person is Jason."

Ken smiled and nodded. "Wus up."

Jason looked him up and down. "So you got yo self another one eh?"

Danielle frowned. "What's that supposed to mean?"

Jason grinned. "Nothing, good luck bruh!"

He then turned and walked toward the house.

She frowned. "I really hate him."

Ken looked at Danielle. "What was that about?"

"He's an idiot."

Ken snickered. "Okay."

"Let's get something to eat."

They continued toward walking until they saw Kima

162

and Deja sitting on lawn chairs with the kids running around playing. Mike was on his rusty grill flipping burgers. Kima connected her phone to a pair of portable speakers and was playing Beyoncé remake of *"Before I Let Go."*

"Hey everybody," Danielle greeted.

A smile spread across Kima's face. "Well it's nice to see you two again."

"Don't burn my burger, Mike," Danielle teased.

"You know better, I'm like the black Bobby Flay on this grill," he bragged.

"Well hurry up and feed me then!" Deja went over to her sister and gave her a hug. She held onto her sister and laid her head on her shoulder. Danielle could tell something was off.

"What's wrong sis?"

"Nothing. I'm okay."

Danielle looked at her. "Are you sure?"

Deja shrugged her shoulders and walked back to her chair. Danielle sat next to Ken and made small talk. She looked up and saw something that shocked her. She thought maybe she had been in the sun too long because what she was seeing was unbelievable. Kurt and Rick were walking up to the cookout side by side laughing with each other as if they had been buddies for years.

"What in the world," she blurted out loud.

The others looked toward where she was looking and couldn't believe it either.

"Is that Rick and Kurt?" Kima asked.

Deja was just as shocked to see them together as the rest but another part of her was happy to see Kurt again. "Yeah it is."

Rick stopped a safe distance away seeing the evil glares he was getting from Danielle.

"Oh shit," he mumbled.

"What?" Kurt looked ahead and saw anger brewing on Danielle's face.

"It's cool dude," Kurt assured. "Don't even trip. C'mon." Kurt grabbed his shoulder in a reassuring fashion insisting that they continue.

Ken was confused by the ladies reaction and turned to Danielle. "What's the problem?"

Instead of answering him, she got up and walked over to Mike. Deja followed behind her.

"What's Rick doing here with Kurt? And since when are they friends?"

"They ran into each other a few days ago at Jason's," he explained. "He apologized and they squashed they beef."

"Rick apologized?" Danielle said with disbelief.

"Yeah. Why is that so hard to believe? They're grown ass men."

"Okay." She huffed. "So what is he doing here?"

Mike looked at her sideways. "I invited him and don't be mean."

"Since when am I mean?"

Mike shook his head then focused his attention on the grill. Jason returned from inside the house and saw Kurt. The look on Deja's face told him things weren't good in paradise. He decided to lay back for a moment to watch what unfolded.

"Give me a minute," Danielle told her sister and walked toward the men.

"Wus up, Dani?" Kurt smiled and gave her a hug.

"Hey you."

An awkward second passed then Kurt spoke up. "Well, I'ma give you two a moment." He bumped fists with Rick and headed toward the grill.

"You two are friends now?" Danielle asked, still shocked at what she saw.

"Yeah. Kurt is actually a good dude."

"I never would've thought."

"People do change, Dani."

She looked at him and changed the subject. "How's

your mom?"

He exhaled deeply. "She's okay. Her doctor didn't like some of her test results and decided to keep her for a few more days."

"Oh wow." Danielle sighed. "Maybe we should get a second opinion."

"You know someone?"

"Yeah, a Cardiologist I used as an expert on a medical malpractice case I worked on last year. His schedule is busy but maybe I can call in a favor and get her worked in sooner than later."

"I'd appreciate that, Dani. Thank you."

She nodded.

Rick could see more than just concern for his mother in her eyes. Even after six years apart he knew her. As much as she pretended not to care about him, her eyes betrayed her. Ken could tell by the way they were looking at each other, there was something between them so he decided to assess the situation himself.

"Hey." Ken interrupted their conversation.

Danielle was slightly startled. She had almost forgotten he was there. "Oh, Rick this is my friend, Ken."

"How you doing," Ken extended his hand.

"Nice to meet you."

The two men evaluated the other and they both realized they wanted the same girl. Kurt walked toward them and Deja's eyes followed him hoping his feelings had healed and she could explain what happened between her and Jason.

"Wus up y'all." Kurt gave Kima a hug and purposely ignored Deja. He then looked at Mike at the grill. "Yo Mike! I know you burning something good over there!"

He walked past Deja toward Mike. Deja sighed knowing his feelings had not changed at all.

Jason was satisfied knowing his plan had worked. Now all he had to do was swoop back in on Deja and things would go back to normal.

"What's going on between you two?" Kima asked, quickly picking up on their exchange.

Deja shook her head. "He found out about Jason."

"What? Oh God. I'm sorry."

"It is what it is, right?" Deja shrugged her shoulders.

Kima put her arm around her while Kurt and Mike stood at the grill chatting. In between chatter, Mike slid a couple of burgers on his plate.

"Hey Kima," Rick called out, looking around the yard, making his way to the grill, "didn't y'all have a cat?"

"Yeah. Snuffles has being missing for a few months."

"Wasn't that cat kinda evil?"

Kima frowned. "I wish you all would stop calling him evil! He was a sweet cat!"

"Didn't he used to kill small animals?" Kurt chimed in. "You know, I read a University study that said if cats were bigger and stronger they would kill you if they could."

"I read that too! They also said if you were to drop dead in your house eventually they'll start eating you."

Kurt pointed at Rick. "That's why I'm a dog person."

Kima glared at them both. "Shut up! I can't stand y'all."

Mike looked around. "Anybody seen Starr?"

Kurt shrugged his shoulders. "She ain't here yet? She's usually the first one."

Mike shook his head. "I think I know why she's late."

Jason made his way to the grill and Kurt glared at him. Jason smiled knowing that he felt some type of way. Rick saw Jason and gave him a man hug then glanced back at Danielle with Ken.

"Everything okay, bruh?" Jason asked.

Rick nodded. "Yeah. Who's the new dude?"

"He's one of Kima's friends. He's a good dude."

Mike stepped away from the grill. "How's your mom, Rick?"

"She's coming along."

Jason turned and picked up Mike's grill fork.

166

"Hey! What do you think you're doing?"

Jason looked at him. "I'm just flipping the steaks."

Mike swiftly took the fork out of his hand. "You aren't ever allowed to touch my grill."

"Why you so sensitive?" Jason laughed knowingly.

"Stay away from my grill."

"What's that all about?" Rick looked at Kurt.

"Oh … you weren't here for mad cow last year."

Rick frowned. "Mad cow?"

"Yep. Mad cow," Mike confirmed then looked at Jason. "Last year I let this fool man the grill for a few minutes while I hit the head. Next thing I know he's serving half cooked burgers to everybody."

"I like my meat with a little pink in the middle." Jason defended his actions and shrugged.

"A little pink?" Mike frowned. "That sucka was still mooing!"

"Yeah okay, but did you die?"

Mike was starting to see red as his left eye twitched. "What the hell kind of question is that? Just stay away from my grill!"

Jason snickered and looked behind Mike. "Instead of worrying about me shouldn't you be doing your annoying big brother thing?"

Mike turned and saw his sister with Darnell standing over by the girls making small talk.

"Kurt, watch the grill."

Mike made his way over to them. He was looking forward to this moment. From the night he talked Darnell at Jason's, he knew he was no good for his sister.

"Hey nice of you both show up."

Starr gave her brother a hug.

"Hey Mike," Darnell acknowledged. "Thanks for extending the invitation to me. I didn't think you wanted me around."

He folded his arms. "Now why wouldn't I want

someone like you around my sister?"

Starr stepped in front of her brother. "Mike, stop it. I know I shoulda told you about Darnell and me sooner but I knew you would act like this."

Everybody stood around watching the siblings square off. It wasn't the first time Mike called out one of Starr's boyfriends. Deja shook her head remembering when she confronted him about Starr's relationship with Tariq.

"This isn't the time or place for this, honey." Kima took his arm.

Mike pulled away. "Oh, I think this is the perfect time babe."

"Oh god here we go!" Starr shook her head. "Here comes the big brother knows best shit."

"I only do because I made a promise to our dad to take care of you."

"When I was a kid!" Starr barked, frustrated. "I'm an adult now!"

"I'm concerned about the men you bring around."

Starr rolled her eyes. "Concerned about what? My dating life? Who I choose to see is my own business! Darnell is a good man."

"A good man you say? How well do you know him?"

"I know him very well," she spat back and stood toe to toe with her brother. "Like I told you before, that's nothing I don't know. Quit trying to come up with shit that's not there!"

Kima had heard enough. "Michael, stop it."

He ignored his wife and continued. "Did he tell you everything about himself?"

Darnell stepped to Mike. "Listen bruh, like I told you the other night the only thing I wanna do with your sister is treat her right. I've been straight up with her."

"Really?" Mike quizzed matter of factly. "About everything?"

"Yes, about everything."

"Even about your criminal history?"

Darnell's mouth dropped completely taken off guard.

"What wrong, bruh? You forgot tell her about that?"

Starr looked at Darnell. "What is he talking about?"

"Babe." Darnell took her hand. "I was going to tell you about this later."

"Tell me about what?" Starr demanded to know.

"About the two years he did in jail for drug possession." Mike answered for Darnell with satisfaction. "I did a little background check on your boy and it popped right up."

Kima put her hand on her head. "Michael, I can't believe you did this."

"Somebody had to. He obviously didn't."

Darnell took Starr's hands. "It's true, I was locked up on drug trafficking charges but there's more to the story than just that."

"Oh you mean the gun possession charge too?" Mike added more fuel to the fire.

Darnell huffed. "It wasn't my gun. That charge was dropped."

"Oh my god!" Starr pulled away. "You should've told me."

She turned and quickly walked toward the house.

"Starr!" Darnell wailed.

Rick and Danielle looked at each other. It was like déjà vu. Darnell shook his head, glared at Mike, and walked away.

"You still on that dumb shit." Deja growled at Mike. "Grow up."

Kima scowled at her husband in disgust. "I hope you're happy."

She turned and headed toward the house.

"Real smooth there, Mikey." Jason shook his head.

"Hey, if he was honest with her this wouldn't have been a problem."

169

"That wasn't cool, bruh." Kurt added.

"Darnell, wait up!" Deja shouted and trotted toward him.

He turned around.

"Hey listen, I know there's more to this. Just let me talk to Starr and work this out."

"Thanks Deja." His eyes darted toward the house then back at her. "I was going to tell her everything. I'm not the same person I was ten years ago."

"Whoa, wait." She did a double take. "Ten years ago?"

"Yes," he confirmed.

Deja rolled her eyes. "I can't believe he did this. Just give her some time."

He nodded and sulked away toward his car. There was tension everywhere. Deja stood quietly wondering why everything had fallen apart. Better yet, she wondered if any of it could it be fixed.

MY CURRENT SITUATION   BY   MARLON MCCAULSKY

Happy Wife Happy Life ... Maybe

UNION CITY - MIKE & KIMA'S HOUSE

Later that night, Mike was in his man cave playing Madden on Xbox. The mood of the cookout after his revelation made things awkward and the festivities ended sooner than later. As far as Mike was concerned, he had done nothing wrong. He knew Starr was pissed at him, but knew she would get over it and thank him later.

"Touchdown," He yelled.

Mike caught his wife glaring at him. He knew what she was going to say but didn't care. So he decided to act like nothing happened.

"Hey babe, the kids in bed?"

"Yep," she dryly replied.

"Good, that's good. I was a little worried about Kennedy eating all that barbeque. You know how sensitive her stomach is."

"Un huh." Kima folded her arms.

Mike could feel his wife's piercing eyes burn a hole in the side of his head.

He sighed. "So are you just gonna give me evil eyes at me all night?

"You just couldn't help yourself could ya?"

"You know as well as I do Starr needed to know the truth."

She walked toward him. "Yes she did but not like that and not from you."

"If not me then who, baby?" He paused for dramatic effect. "I've always had my sister's best interest at heart."

Kima shook her head. "You just don't get it?"

"Get what?"

"That your sister is not a little girl. She's twenty seven years old."

172

Mike tossed the game controller on the sofa. "So what? Does that mean I stop being her brother? If I see a bus about to hit her I'm going to push her out the way."

"I love that you love her like that but you go way too far!"

"I do what I have to," Mike mumbled.

"You know I've warned you if keep this up you're going to push her away."

"We'll be okay. Starr needs me. She doesn't always make good choices."

"And neither does her brother." She looked at him and shook her head. "Good night."

~~~

A couple of hours passed by and Mike was tired of playing Madden. He figured he had given Kima enough time to calm down and was ready to slip into bed, spoon up next to that nice round ass then get back to work on making that third child. Mike darted upstairs and turned the knob on his bedroom door but it was locked.

"Kima." He knocked. "Kima, babe the door. The door is locked."

"I know," she confirmed. "I locked it."

"C'mon babe," he whined, "just open the door and let's talk."

"Nah, that's okay, I'm good."

"Don't be like that." He turned the knob again.

"Mike, I love you but I really don't want to look at you right now."

His brow crinkled. "Seriously? Kima... babe!"

"Don't wake up the kids."

He huffed. "You're over reacting."

"Good night, Michael."

"Kima, honey? Babe?"

She gave him no answer. Over the years he's gotten

the silent treatment from her and knew she wasn't gonna give in any time soon.

"Okay... alright." He sighed. "I'ma sleep in the spare room. All by myself. Alone. Missing you."

He slowly walked to the other room. Kima had never locked him out before. Maybe he did go too far this time. Maybe.

MY CURRENT SITUATION   BY   MARLON MCCAULSKY

Bruh

In life you meet a lot of people. Some people become your friends others become acquaintances. But the bond they shared was deeper. No matter how much time passed or miles stood between them, they were family and never lost contact with each other.

After the cookout, Rick and Jason went to the hospital to see his mom. Sharon was happy to see her boys together again. She was always glad Rick had Jason in his life growing up. They needed each other. As always, Jason was able to put a smile on her face. After a while Sharon grew tired and the fellas decided to let her rest and they headed to Jason's Lounge to shoot some pool.

Jason leaned over the table and shot the solid colored number four ball into the corner pocket. "You know your Mom is gonna be okay, right? She's strong. No need to stress about it."

Rick was standing to the side holding his cue stick. "I know she is. It's just hard but I'll get through it."

"I know how you feel." He exhaled. "I hate seeing her like that."

"Yeah, there are so many things I wish I could do differently." He paused, taking in thought. "Maybe moving to LA was a mistake."

Jason shot and missed his target. "Don't beat yourself up. You had a great opportunity and your Mom would've killed you if you didn't take it."

"She sure would have."

Rick took aim with his cue stick and sunk the number six ball in the side pocket. Jason took chugged the beer he had on the table behind them as Rick worked the table.

Rick sunk another ball. "Anyway, on another note,

what's up with Mike? It seems like he's gotten worse over the years when it comes to Starr."

Jason sighed. "Yeah, he's straight up buggin' yo. I'm surprised she has any kind of dating life with him around."

Rick missed his shot. "You know when we were younger I got it. That's his sister. He didn't want dudes trying to run up in her; but damn, you gotta let her live. I'm surprised she ain't still a virgin. So is your boy okay?"

"Yeah he texted me while we were at the hospital. He's pissed. He was really feeling her."

"So did you know about his past?"

Jason took his shot and knocked in the striped six ball in the side pocket.

"Yeah, he told me. Had I known Mike would go all CSI on him I woulda gave him a heads up. That's why love ain't for everybody."

Rick gave a knowing head nod. "Is that why you went out of your way to shit on Kurt and Deja's relationship?"

Jason laughed. "What you talking about, bruh?"

"You know what I'm talking about. All that wild shit you were talking about Deja. You know!"

Jason laughed some more. "Oh that. Hey I was sharing with the fellas."

"You were trying to piss Kurt off. You knew they were together. That was some foul shit, Jay, even for you."

"What's that supposed to mean? Even for me?" He stared at Rick. "Like I do shit all the time."

"Remember in eighth grade when you lost your starting position on the basketball team to Louis Stevenson?"

"Lou… ol' Louie. Yeah, I remember that freakishly long legged, Akeem Elijahwan looking mutha—." He caught himself. "What about him?"

"Remember you put that itching powder shit in his jockstrap?"

"Whatever." He shrugged. "He's the only dude I knew who wore a jockstrap. That shit was funny!"

"Yeah, it was, but that was some vindictive shit. You were in your feelings about losing your spot. Same way you must have been feeling when you found out about Deja and Kurt." Rick leaned back against the wall. "I didn't know you and Deja had a thing. You feeling her like that?"

"Nah." He shrugged his shoulders. "We just hooked up one night, decided we liked it and kept it going. Nobody knew. No commitment just sex." He looked at Rick. "But whatever, she wanted to fuck with Kurt; I just thought he should know."

Rick shook his head. "You mean you felt some type of way and decided to blow shit up. Typical Jason."

He couldn't even deny that Rick figured him out. Ever since he lost Selena years ago Jason made a point not to catch feelings for any woman again. He let his guard down with Deja. "If you say so."

Jason went back to shooting pool.

"You wrong bruh, you dead wrong. I could see it on Deja's face today. She's was really feeling him."

"Well, if they broke up simply because I dropped some truth, then it must have not been all that!" Jason surmised truthfully.

"You better be careful messing with Kurt. "He warned. "He got a mean right hook, trust me."

"I ain't worried about him but you should be concerned about Dani's new boy toy."

"Ken?"

"Yeah." He nodded. "He look like one of them smooth talking, get the panties moist, Larenz Tate, make you an omelet in the morning after I hit it looking muthafuckas. If you gonna get her back, you gonna need to act fast before he get them draws. And don't stand there and say you don't want her back. I know you do."

"If Dani wants to be with me again she ain't telling me."

Jason gave him the side eye. "You think she gonna

178

make it easy for you? Bruh, for the last six years she's had it out for you. She's gonna make you work for that ass again."

"So let me get this straight, you're not against me getting back with her even after you went out of your way to drive it through my head that we were moving too fast. Now you're cool with it?"

Jason stared at him. "Bruh, we ain't kids anymore. Both of you are grown now and she's one for you. Everybody knows that. You do too."

Sisterly Advice

After the cookout, Danielle ventured out to Deja's apartment that evening to check on her. She walked to up to her apartment door and knocked. Seconds later Deja opened door, smiled, and gave her a hug.

"Are you okay," Danielle asked.

"I'm okay."

"I've been calling and texting. You never responded."

"Sorry, my phone died and I just didn't bother to charge it."

Danielle sat on the couch and could tell by Deja's tone and body language she was feeling some type of way. Normally Deja would be upbeat and talkative instead she was a bit aloof. She wasn't beaming with joy like she was a few days ago at Kima's house.

"Okay, now I know something is wrong. I could tell something was up with you at the barbeque. What's going on?"

Deja fidgeted momentarily debating if she should tell her. "Dani, I don't wanna bother you with my problems."

"It's okay, I wanna know."

"Well." Deja sighed. "I wasn't going to tell you because I wasn't sure how you would react but I guess now it doesn't matter."

"What is it?" Danielle looked at her sister with concern in her eyes.

"For the last couple of weeks, ah, I've been seeing Kurt."

A big smile spread across Danielle's face. "What! Are you serious?"

Deja nodded.

Danielle was absolutely shocked. Kurt? After all the

years of them being friends, he ends up hooking up with her sister? She always knew he liked her but she had no idea Deja was even interested. "Why didn't you wanna tell me?"

Deja shrugged her shoulders. "We weren't sure how you would take it and honestly I didn't think you would approve of me being with him."

"Why would you think that?"

"I just know you think I'm a bad influence and he's is a good guy."

Danielle leaned forward. "Is that what you think I think of you?"

"Well yeah. You always criticize the men I date."

"That's because they're losers, but Kurt, he's a good man. He's actually the kind of man you should be with."

Deja was visibly surprised. "Really?"

"Yes!" Danielle grinned from ear to ear.

"Well, I kinda have another confession. For the past couple of months I've been hooking up with Jason."

Danielle smile turned into a frown. "What! Eww! Why?"

"C'mon Dani, I know you hate his guts but he's kinda fine."

"If you say so. You see, this is why I call the dudes you date losers. Of all the guys ..." Danielle paused and realized what she was doing. What she's always done. Judging her instead of being there for her. She could see the annoyed look on Deja's face. "Okay, never mind. My feelings about Jason are irrelevant. So what happened between you and Kurt?"

"I don't know how but he found out about me and Jason and ended it." A tear fell from her eye.

"You mean he didn't already know about y'all?"

"No."

"Okay, so I'm confused. You were with Jason before Kurt, so why would he end things because of that?"

Deja looked up at the ceiling and shook her head at

the memory. "The first night I was supposed to go out with him, Jason came over and I stood him up."

"Deja, you didn't."

"I know, I know, I fucked up! I just want to know how he found out about it."

"From who else?" Danielle huffed. "Jason!"

"You think so?"

Danielle gave a knowing look. "Who else would it be?"

"But why would he tell Kurt anything? It's not like we were serious."

"It doesn't matter. They talk more than we do. Men are really like dogs. They act like they don't care but they don't wanna see another man playing with their bone."

Deja shook her head. "I really liked him, Dani. We really connected."

Danielle could tell Deja was really saddened by all of this. She had never seen her like this over a man. She took her hand. "Well if you really feel like you had a connection with him give him some time to come around. He's hurt right now. You know how a man's ego is."

Deja nodded. "Yeah okay."

"Hey cheer up, your birthday is next week," Danielle reminded her.

"I really don't feel like celebrating it."

Danielle's eyes widened like saucers. "You don't wanna celebrate your day? Damn girl, you really must be heartbroken! Was the dick that good?"

Deja smiled at her bougie sister. "I just can't believe the one time I fall for a good guy I mess it up."

Danielle hugged her. "It's not over Deja, trust me." The two continued chatting for a couple of hours reconnecting as sisters. Danielle was really amazed at Deja's new found maturity. She actually felt comfortable opening up to her. It was truly like a new beginning for them. Even as improbable of a couple they were to her, she really hoped things worked out between Deja and Kurt. If they could get past their issues who knows what else could happen?

Drunk and No Love

BUCKHEAD - JASON'S LOUNGE

She moved her body on the dance floor like she had graduated top of her class at Magic City. She allowed her body to be controlled by the beat and swayed her hips from side to side. Her body was slightly damp from perspiration on the dance floor. The Honey Jack Daniels and Sprite in her system made her feel looser. She could feel the hardness in his jeans as she grinded her backside against him. She smiled, pleased that she was able to evoke such raw lust. This was a side Danielle rarely showed in public, a side that Ken was thrilled to be on the receiving end of.

The song switched and she spun around and faced him. She put her body against his hard muscular frame. She wanted him to feel her. The skimpy black dress she wore didn't put much in between them. Only a strapless bra underneath prevented her hard nipples from making an unscheduled appearance. She had made up her mind that she was going give herself to him tonight. It had been too long since she felt a man inside of her, and judging what she felt in his jeans, Ken had a lot to give.

"You feel so good," he whispered in her ear.

"You do too."

"I didn't know you could dance like that."

"There's a lot you don't know yet." She slyly grinned.

"I can't wait to find out."

"I need another drink."

Ken kissed her neck, took her hand, and led her to the bar where he ordered another Jack and Sprite. He watched as her perfect lips pressed up against the glass and wanted to taste them again. Danielle glanced up and caught his lustful eyes on her. She liked it. She leaned in and kissed him. Her head felt light. His kiss was intoxicating. Or maybe that was the Jack. Either way she liked the way he was making

184

her feel.

ATLANTA - DANIELLE'S CONDO

Before she knew it she was in the passenger side of his car speeding down the highway toward the Skyrise Condos near Atlantic Station. She leaned back in the seat staring lustfully at Ken's handsome face while he drove. His free hand caressing her thigh made her feel hot. She imagined every nasty thing she was going to do to him tonight. Once he pulled into the parking garage of her condo they made their way to the elevator. Danielle was noticeably wobbly but kept her balance.

They rode up to the eighteenth floor and were all over each other. He could still taste the Honey Jack on her tongue. His hands explored her body finding a resting place on her soft ass. Before they could go any further they both heard a "ding" letting them know they reached her floor. They playfully exited the elevator holding hands.

Danielle led him to her door, pulled her key out from her wristlet, unlocked the door and went inside. Once the door closed, she pulled him close and kissed him. Passionately. Forcefully. Hungrily. Ken returned her lustful kiss. There would be no love making tonight, strictly back braking. Ken hoisted her up by her ass, took her to the sofa, and laid her down. Danielle lifted his shirt over his head revealing his muscular body. She liked it. He kissed her again. His hand feeling her thighs. Sliding up under her dress, he moved her panties to the side and touched her, driving her crazy. Moistness covered his fingers. Soft moans escaped her lips as he caressed her. His head went down between her thighs. She bit her bottom lip anticipating the things Ken would do to her. Danielle wanted to be taken in every kind of way.

"Yesssssss ... don't stop," she moaned.

His tongue tasted her clit. She closed her eyes and her body trembled. Another uncontrollable moan left her lips.

She raised her behind up allowing him to slowly pull her panties down. Once he removed them, he went back down in her valley. Ken wasn't sloppy. He was precise and focused as he licked her into bliss. It had been years since a man had gone down on her. Her body trembled as her head fell back. Ken assaulted her clit, lick after lick until she couldn't hold back anymore.

"Don't stop, Rick!"

Suddenly, everything stopped. Ken froze. Danielle opened her eyes. She realized her mistake. Her mind and tongue betrayed her. She didn't know what to do. Ken slowly rose up from between her legs and Danielle pushed up on her elbows.

"Well, that's the first time that's ever happened to me."

"Ken, I am so sorry. I didn't mean to. It was a mistake."

"It's okay."

Danielle had a disappointed look on her face. "No, it's not. I feel horrible. It was a mistake a stupid mistake!"

"Dani, Dani, calm down."

"I can make this up to you." She leaned forward and kissed him again. "I can prove it."

Ken pulled away. "It's okay. You don't to have prove anything to me. I want you. You're an incredible woman and so beautiful." He caressed her face. "I don't wanna just have sex with you. You're the kind of woman I want to build something with but I can't do that when you're in love with somebody else."

Danielle's mouth fell open. "In love? No! I'm not! It was years ago and it's over between us. Long over!"

"Really now?" He quizzed. "I saw the way you looked at each other. Something was still there. I didn't know how strong it still was until now."

Ken got up and put his shirt back on.

"Where are you going?"

"Home." He looked at her. "I think it's best for no until you really figure out what you feel."

She exhaled as he walked to door. He turned and looked at her. "Take care."

He opened the door and left. Danielle sunk back into the sofa, closed her eyes and cursed. *What the hell is wrong with me*, she thought. Why did she say his name? Of all the times to have a mental slip. She was angry and still horny. A deadly combination. She got up, marched to the kitchen and grabbed a bottle of wine from the fridge. Unscrewing the cap, she poured a glass and quickly downed it. She was pissed. She had never made a slip up like that before even when she was purposely thinking about somebody else. She took another drink, glanced up and saw her car keys on the counter.

~~~

AVONDALE ESTATES - MS. SHARON'S HOUSE

Somehow sleeping in your childhood bed as an adult feels odd. The room always seems too small. Maybe it was everything he had on his mind that made it hard for Rick to sleep. He tossed and turned until the sandman came. The doorbell erupted in a frantic concussion of ringing. He jumped out of his sleep, alarmed. Quickly, Rick stumbled out of bed half naked except for a pair of red boxer briefs. The ringing continued as he rushed down the stairs. Rick arrived at the door and looked though the peep hole. He couldn't believe she was on his doorstep. Her eyes were glazed over but she was still sexy.

"What the," He opened the door. "Dani?"

"What the hell are you doing here?"

Rick looked around a bit confused. "I ... live here."

She stared at him for a second. He had a point but nevertheless she continued, "I know that!"

"Are you drunk?"

She barged by him and entered the house.

"Don'tcha try and ... and change the subject," she slurred.

"Dani, you drove drunk over here? Are you insane? You could've killed yourself! Or somebody else!"

"Shut up! Just shut your ... smug little face! You ... you don't get to talk to me like that! I'm askin' the questions here! What are you doing back here!"

Rick exhaled. "What? Dani, you know why I'm back here. My mom."

She then remembered. "Shit ... Why are you back in my life? I ... I was doing so fine before you came back. Why?"

"I don't understand. What did I do?"

"You ruined everything! I can't get your stupid face out my mind! And because of you I fucked things up with Ken! Because of you!"

Rick was confused. How did he ruin anything between her and Ken? He stepped toward her. "Dani, I'm sorry."

"Stop apologizing! I hate you!" She punched his chest. Rick took her blow. "I hate your guts!" She swung again franticly.

"Stop," He yelled and grabbed her arms. "Stop it!"

She continued to struggle then stopped when she looked into his eyes. Rick relaxed his grip on her arms. Danielle inhaled his scent; then did the unexpected—she kissed him. Rick was shocked but returned her kiss. For six years this was they what they both wanted. Their passion exploded. Danielle's hands explored his body while Rick's arms held her close. They pulled away slowly and exchanged smiles. It was a drunk smile but still sexy. Just as she was going to kiss him again she felt something vile. Her eyes widened like saucers. Rick saw the look on her face and thought she was going to hit him again.

"Dani, are you okay?"

She quickly covered her mouth, ran to the bathroom, and threw up.

Rick shook his head. "Figures."

He went to the bathroom and saw her hugging the bowl. "How much did you have to drink?"

"Just a little." She felt another surge come up her throat and gave her insides to the bowl again. Rick pulled her hair back. "Okay, maybe more than a little."

"C'mon let me help you."

Rick walked her to the spare bedroom downstairs. She could barely put one foot in front of another. He was still shocked that she made it to his place in one piece. Her kiss was still on his mind. He laid her down in the bed and pulled the covers over her. Danielle quickly gave into the darkness and fell asleep. Rick stared at the woman he loved. After all these years she was in his bed again. Well sorta. He was relieved there was still something there. He smiled and quietly left the room.

Hours later, Danielle's eyes fluttered. It felt like she had a cement block sitting on her forehead. Her stomach turned. She felt drained, dehydrated, and hung the fuck over. She was in no condition to go anywhere right now. She looked around the room, the surroundings were familiar. She had spent a lot of her younger years in this room with Rick. Coming over late nights and making out with him while his mother was asleep. Good memories of happier times. Then she heard a knock on the door.

Rick opened the door and walked in with a cup of coffee in his hand. "Hey there."

She nodded.

He handed her the cup and she took a sip. "Thank you."

"How do you feel?" He sat on the side of the bed next to her.

"Like a fool." She looked at him. "We didn't ..."

He smiled. "No, we didn't."

"How long have I been out?" She touched her head.

"About twelve hours give or take."

"I'm sorry."

"It's okay. I've done worse when I was drunk."

"I feel like idiot. I didn't mean what I said last night."

"Oh, you remember?"

She remembered attacking Rick then kissing him. She also recalled making out with Ken and saying Rick's name. Things she would have never done in her right mind. She felt like a bit of hoe.

"Vaguely." She drank more of the coffee.

It's okay, I deserved some of it."

"No you didn't. I acted like a jackass." She looked at him. "Thank you for taking care of me."

"I always will." He took her hand and they looked into each other's eyes. "About what happened last night, I realized you were drunk and you didn't mean most of it. I'm not going to hold it over your head."

Danielle looked at him.

"But I know a part of you wanted it to happen and I'm glad it did."

She didn't know what to say. She couldn't deny it. Rick got up from the bed. "You can rest here as long as you want."

She nodded. "Thank you."

If You Think You're Lonely Now

ATLANTA - DEJA'S APARTMENT

It was the night before Memorial Day and Jason was just a couple of blocks away from Deja's apartment. He was thrilled to get a text from her asking if he wanted to come over. His plan to mess up Kurt's connection with her had worked. Now things could go back to normal he figured and their hook ups would become more steady. The sex he had with her was off the hook and he was in need of some that good stuff. He parked in the parking lot and made his way to her apartment door and rang the bell.

The door opened and big grin spread across his face seeing Deja dressed in a black lace teddy that could barely contain all of her thickness. Her ample cleavage looked like two ripe honey dew melons and his mouth watered. Deja wore her hair cascading down her shoulders. Her nails and toes were painted pink and her makeup flawless. Jason knew in his mind that he was going to tear her ass up like never before.

"Good lawd," he murmured biting his lower lip.

Deja smiled. "Hey Jay, how you doing?"

"I'm doing a hell of lot better now that I see you!"

"You missed me?"

"Like a fat kid miss cake!" He looked her up and down hungrily.

He attempted to go inside but Deja stopped him.

"Wus up, boo?" He asked, confused.

"Before I let you come … inside," she teased. "I need to know one thing."

"Just say the word." His dick jumped looking at her.

Deja's smile morphed into something angry. "Why did you tell Kurt about us?"

Jason's face dropped. "Say what?"

192

"You heard me, why did you tell Kurt about us?"

Jason felt Deja's eyes burning a hole through him and his hardness turned flaccid. She could see the guilt on his face as he tried to think of a lie. Danielle was right, it was Jason that told him. He was flustered and decided to confess.

"It might have come up," he admitted.

Deja frowned. "It might have come up? That was only supposed to stay between us!"

Jason huffed. "It slipped out."

"We been kickin' it for months now and all of a sudden it just slipped outta your mouth, to him of all people?"

"So you feeling him now? You in love or something," he asked sarcastically.

Deja glowered. "Doesn't matter how I feel about him. The big question is how did you even know?"

Jason shook his head. "What's that gotta do with what me and you got going on?"

Deja wanted punch him in his face. "Why did you tell him? Were you on some jealous type of shit?"

"Of Kurt, please! I know he can't do you like I do."

"Oh, is that what you think?" Deja folded her arms across her chest.

"That's what I know." Jason shot back with arrogance.

"For the record," Deja touched her crotch, "Kurt puts his name all over my kitty kat again and again and again. He knows how to treat a woman. Not just fuck!"

"Well you sure didn't have a problem getting fucked and quite well I might add. So now you wanna be held and shit? Now you want romance? Whatever Deja. We both know once you get tired of holding hands with that loser you'll want that old thang back." He held his crotch.

"I wouldn't fuck you again if you were the last dick on Earth."

"Really?" He smirked. "Who you kidding?"

"Hold up … you hear that?"

Jason looked around. "Hear what?"

She cuffed her ear. "This."

Deja slammed the door in his face. Jason couldn't believe he went to her place for her to play him. He was horny and ready to get it in.

"Deja!" He pounded on the door. "Stop playing! C'mon man! Alright! Be like that! See if I care!"

Moody

In the past few days after her drunken escapade, Danielle found herself inexplicably irritable. Messing things up with Ken and kissing Rick put her in a mood. She was starting to feel things for him she thought she had expelled from her heart years ago. Even though she felt certain things coming back she refused to give him another chance to break her heart.

She decided to throw Deja a birthday party at her condo in two days but first she need to make sure a very important guest would show up. She pulled up to Kurt's house and parked. Moments later, he greeted her after knocking on his door. Kurt smiled seeing his friend.

"Hey you."

"Dani? Hey, what are you doing here?"

"I just came by to see you."

"Really? Come in." He stepped to the side. "Can I get you something to drink?"

She had a seat on the sofa. "No, I'm good. I love your house. Your realtor hooked you up."

"Well my realtor is my cousin, Joyce Roland. She went above and beyond to find this place for me. "Kurt sat next to her. "So what's going on with you?"

Danielle's neck craned. "Why you always assuming I wanna talk about my life?"

"Because you usually do." He told her truthfully. "You're predictable."

"Man whatever!" She smiled and gave him the middle finger. "Anyway, I came by to talk about you."

"What about me?"

"Why have you been acting like such a dick to Deja? I know you like her."

Kurt was taken off guard by her question. The whole situation with Deja was sort of unexpected and he didn't want Danielle to find out in case things didn't work out. But the cat was out of the bag now, he reckoned.

"So she told you?"

"Yep." She smiled. "I thought you were gonna wait for me."

He looked at her seriously. "Don't start that, Dani."

"Okay, okay, okay, I was just playing with you! But on the real, why have you been so rude to my sister?"

Kurt sucked his teeth. "Did she tell you everything?"

"You mean about her and Jason?"

Kurt frowned. "You knew?"

"Yes, after she told me."

"At least she told you. I had to find out from that fool bragging about how many different times he fucked her! She shoulda told me about that shit ahead of time!"

"Because you've told her about every chick you done hit right," Danielle responded, sarcastically.

"It's not the same." Kurt rubbed his head. "She don't know any of the chicks I been with before but she knew I hung out with Jason."

"That's exactly why she didn't tell you right away. She really likes you and didn't want to hurt your feelings."

Kurt shook his head. "Well, how did that work out for her?"

"Why you acting like such a girl? You already knew about her colorful past and that's awkward enough. She was just embarrassed to tell you because of how she would look in your eyes."

"Still man, she shoulda told me."

"Ok, but she didn't. Look at this way, she's choosing you over Jay. Obviously you did something a lot better than he did which I don't need any details on. Anyway, I'm throwing a birthday party for her at my place Saturday night." She stood up. "If you decide to man up, come by. I know she wants to see you."

"Damn Dani, I thought I was the one who was supposed to be blunt and to the point. When did you get so hardcore?"

"I learned it from you." She gave him a hug. "See you Saturday."

Danielle left. Kurt shook his head and couldn't do anything but laugh. He hated to admit it but she was right.

~~~

UNION CITY - MIKE & KIMA'S HOUSE

Across town, the cold war was still very much in effect between Mike and Kima. She was only talking to him when she had to, no matter how bad he tried to make conversation. She allowed him to sleep in their bedroom but no contact was made. Project baby-making was on indefinite hold.

Mike was growing tired of it. Four days. Kima had never been mad at him for this long. It felt like he was walking on egg shells in his own house. He was glad Kennedy and Kimberly were still too young to pick up on the tension between mommy and daddy, at least he hoped so. He pulled into the driveway, parked and sat there. This was ridiculous. This argument wasn't even about them. This was between him and Starr, who was also giving him the cold shoulder. She hadn't returned any of his calls or texts since the barbeque.

Why is she mad at me? Darnell was the one lying to her, he surmised. He was just the one to bring the truth to light. That's what he kept on telling himself. It was getting harder each time he said it. He remembered the look on Starr's face. Even though Darnell lied, he was the one who caused his sisters pain. It was a guilt he couldn't deny.

Mike got out of his truck and went into the house.

Baked chicken was in the air. He went into the kitchen and watched his wife at the island whipping up a miracle. Kima glanced up at him. Truth was she was just as tired of giving her husband the silent treatment as he was receiving it. She loved him but he had to learn a lesson. For years she had warned him to stay out of his sister's love life. Kima knew if she allowed him to carry on unchecked that one day he would do the same to their daughters.

"Hey babe," Mike greeted.

She nodded.

"Girls are upstairs?"

She looked at him. "Yeah."

She went back to chopping carrots.

"Baby, you were right ... I went too far."

She stopped chopping and looked up at him.

"I'm gonna fix this thing with Starr."

She laid the knife down on the counter. "How?"

"I don't know yet but I can't have you mad at me anymore. I've been miserable."

"You realize what you did to her? You realize how much pain she's in?"

He nodded. "Yeah." He nodded. "I do now."

She walked around the island and stood in front of him.

"Mike, I know what your sister means to you but you have got to let go."

"I know. I just never wanted to let my dad down."

Kima caressed his face. "Your dad would be proud of you but even he would tell you it's time."

He nodded. "What about us? Are we okay now?"

"If someone told me five years ago you would be this aggravating and hard headed, I would still marry your ass."

She kissed him.

A Special Request

ATLANTA - DEJA'S APARTMENT

Deja stood in her bedroom looking over the outfit she had on. It was a black and white striped dress that stopped mid-thigh, a small tan jacket with nude three inch heels that highlighted her sexy thick calves. She was getting ready for her birthday party at Danielle's house. After everything she did to her she was happy she was still willing to do this for her. Part of her still felt depressed that Kurt was still not talking to her. She realized whatever they had, or whatever it could have been, was now over and there was nothing she could do but move on.

She heard her doorbell ring and knew it was her ride. She had already decided she was going to drink like a fish tonight and didn't want to get pulled over with a DUI or worse so she asked the one person she knew who wouldn't get tore up. She opened the door and saw her girl, Starr, looking flawless in a red mini romper.

"Look at you sexy momma!"

"As always, look at you!" Starr looked her up and down. "Looking like you know some dude is gonna wanna see you in your birthday suit tonight!"

She faked a smile knowing that the only man she wanted to show off her birthday suit to was Kurt. "Well, if I get enough drinks in me tonight who knows."

Deja stared at her friend. She was so busy feeling sorry for herself that she almost forgot about the situation she was going through.

"How are you doing?"

Starr shrugged. "I'm fine."

"Have you spoken to Darnell?"

"No." She sighed. "I really don't have anything left to say to him."

"I understand why you're mad. He didn't tell you everything about himself." She paused and reflected on her situation with Kurt. "Trust me, I've made the same mistake."

"So were you a former drug dealer?"

"I'm not saying he wasn't wrong for not telling you everything but maybe you should hear him out. I know you still care about him."

Starr was tired of talking about Darnell. "You ready to go?"

"Yeah, let me go grab my bag." Deja turned around and went to the bedroom. "You know he's going to be at the party tonight?"

Starr looked at her shocked. "Why?"

"Because I invited him. You need to hear him out."

"Why would you do that?" Starr rolled her eyes.

"Because, I'm your friend."

~~~

ATLANTA - DANIELLE'S CONDO

The party had already started and there were about twenty people lounging and talking to each other while Danielle played music from her Apple Music playlist. Danielle made sure to invite all of Deja's close friends. This was the first thing she had gonna out of her way to do for her in years and she wanted it to be an enjoyable night.

In order to keep the atmosphere of the party more of a fun gathering than a wild night at the strip club she decided to hook up her Wii to the flat screen so folks could play Wii Sports or Dance Dance Revolution. Her idea was a success as she observed Mike playing a bowling game with Kima and two others. She looked at her phone and saw a text from Starr letting her know she was on her way with Deja. Danielle decided to dress in a green and purple dress that fell just above her knees with a pair of three inch wedges with the same color scheme as her dress. She had always felt comfortable with her fashion sense.

Darnell and Jason stood to the side checking out some of the pretty ladies. A few of who they already had been with but there were a few new faces among the crowd.

"Oh by the power of Grayskull, would you look at that ass on shorty in the red." Jason pointed out. "I recognize her. She's a YouTuber ...Taylor Fenty. I've been wanting to tap that ass for a while now. Didn't know she was friends with Deja."

Darnell focused his attention on the five-foot-two beauty who was standing next to the couch with her back turned to them looking at the TV screen. She turned her head, glanced back at him and gave him a full on smile. Taylor had been friends with Deja since college and was fully aware of who Jason was as well as his reputation. She wasn't interested in being another notch on his belt but was amused by the attention he was giving her.

"Yeah shorty mean," Darnell confirmed giving Jason some dap.

"I do hanker for a chunk of her cheese umm, know what I mean, Vern? That's why I always loved being friends with Kima and Starr they always got some bad ass freaks around."

Darnell looked at Jason. "So is that why you never tried to holla at her?"

"Yeah, that and I respect Mike too much to put his sister through the JT Experience," he admitted smoothly. "Plus she knows all my tricks and tactics too well."

Darnell laughed at his friend. "How she figure them out?"

"She used to see me and Mike back in high school all the time running game on all them bitches." He reminisced. "She knows the game and was off limits."

"I understand," Darnell agreed. "Same way the situation with Deja and Kurt should have been off limits."

"Aw man, whatever." Jason shoo'd him not wanting

to hear what he was saying.

"Real talk, you know that shit you said was foul, Jay. You know they're not together because of that."

"Why is everybody so anxious to see them together? Did it not occur to you that maybe they wasn't meant to be together? That maybe I did them both a favor and stopped them from making a big mistake?"

Darnell couldn't believe what Jason just said. "Yeah bruh, you keep on telling yourself that and you just might believe it. Sounds like you feeling some type of way."

"For who? Deja?" He laughed. "I already had my fun with that."

Jason was still pissed off at the way she played him a few days ago. He would never admit to Darnell that he was in his feelings about her. Just then the front door opened and in walked Deja and Starr. Darnell licked his lips seeing Starr in a red romper. He was dying to see her again so he could explain the full story of his incarceration at such a young age.

Jason's eyes followed Deja. "Got damn, she's fine. I should hit that ass one last time."

"You're an ambitious man," Darnell joked.

Danielle made her way over to her sister with Kima by her side. "Happy birthday Deja," she sang.

"Thank you so much for doing all of this for me."

The two hugged. "That what sisters do."

"So are we still going out to the club later," Kima blurted out.

Danielle looked at her and laughed. "Yes girl, we're going to the club."

Mike walked over to them. "Happy birthday Deja."

She gave him a hug. Deja looked around a little bit more and noticed that Kurt was not there. She exhaled, faked a smile and thanked everyone around her. Mike returned with drinks, she took hers and went and sat in a love seat near the TV so she could watch the matchup between Kima and Danielle. As she was watching them play Jason walked up to her.

"Happy birthday, Deja!" Jason acknowledged with a smile when he walked up to her.

Her face twisted in disgust. "Go kill ya'self."

"Alrighty then." Jason turned and walked away.

Starr walked toward the bathroom down the hall but before she could go inside she felt someone take her hand. She turned and saw Darnell. Quickly, she turned and looked to see where her brother was. Fortunately, he wasn't looking their direction.

"What are you doing?"

"Follow me," he told her, walking further down the hall.

Starr sighed, looked to see if anybody was watching them, then followed him into an empty room. Once inside she closed the door behind her.

"Darnell ..."

He stepped in front of her, pulled her body close to him and kissed her.

Starr kissed him back enjoying his aggressive behavior. Then she felt his hand go underneath her romper rubbing her butt. She groaned, became moist, feeling his fingers rubbing her the right way. He pulled her toward the bed then pulled her panties to the side and rubbed two fingers over her clit. Her body was dying for this sexual release more than anything else and grinded on his fingers. It wasn't even her birthday and Darnell wanted to lick icing off her cake. She wanted him as much as he wanted her. She was in love with this man. She wanted sex but needed the truth more than that.

"Hold on." She grabbed his hand.

"What?"

"We can't do this." Starr sighed. "Nothing's changed between us."

"I'm sorry. I never meant to lie to you."

Starr shook her head. "But you did. I was really embarrassed thinking I knew everything about you and taking up for you."

He kissed her again. "I can explain everything to you. I promise."

She shook her head and removed his fingers from her sex. "Don't make promises you can't keep."

"I'm not. I swear, Starr, I can make everything clear."

She pulled away from him, adjusted her panties and straightened out her romper. She stared at him for a moment. Her heart wanted to believe him but he lied to her. And as much as her heart wanted to look past it a part of her kept on telling her that if lied to her once, he'll lie to her again. She then turned, walked to door and left Darnell in the room.

"Hey sis!" Mike greeted as he was headed to the bathroom.

Starr glared at her brother and walked by him without saying a word. Mike shook his head. Maybe his wife was right maybe he pushed her too far this time. She's never been this pissed at him before. Just then, Darnell exited from the same room Starr came from. Both men stared at each other for a second then Darnell walked by him without a word.

A partygoer went out the front door to take a call and in walked Kurt with Rick right behind him before the door closed. Kurt spotted Deja playing on the Wii. Both he and Rick made their way through the small crowd to where Mike and Jason were on the other side of the room. Kurt felt a surge of anger seeing Jason but kept his feelings under control.

"What's up fellas," Rick greeted, giving both Mike and Jason some dap.

Kurt did the same.

"So what's going on?" Rick looked around.

"Nothing much," Mike confirmed. "Dani got drinks in the kitchen."

"Cool."

Kurt looked around the room and watched Deja. He thought to himself how stupid he was acting. The way she looked in her short dress could make any man shed a tear. He wanted to get her attention but didn't just wanna march over to her and interrupt her game. After the talk he had with Danielle he felt like an idiot for treating Deja the way he had. He looked back around at Jason and could understand why he did what he did. He wanted him out of the way so he could have Deja for himself.

Jason grinned. "So what's going on, Kurt? You see something here you like?"

Both Rick and Mike looked at Jason as if warning him not to go any further down this road. Jason could feel the "fuck you" vibe coming from Kurt but didn't care.

"As a matter fact I do. Yo, I'ma get a drink." Kurt walked off like a man on a mission.

He realized that he allowed Jason to play him. Deja had chosen him over Jason and he let her go because of his pride. He wondered how he could have been so stupid.

"Hey Dani."

She smiled. "Hey Kurt! You made it!"

"Yeah, I did, and you were right about everything."

"I know." She giggled. "Deja is over on the Wii."

"I saw her." Kurt paused for a moment, pulled out his phone and opened his playlist. "Hey, do you mind if I do something special for her?"

"Of course not! What you wanna do?"

He handed her his phone, told her his plan and walked out of the kitchen.

Deja was enjoying herself when she heard the music in the room stop. Everybody turned to where the speakers were and saw Danielle standing next to it. "Hey everybody I got a special request to play a song for the birthday girl," she announced.

Deja smiled nervously. "You do? From who?"

"Me." Kurt emerged from the hallway.

Deja's heart sped up a beat. She couldn't believe he was there. Seeing him looking good caused an uncontrollable smile to spread across her face. Jason rolled his eyes at how over the top he was being. Kurt stood in the middle of the living room his eyes locked on his prize.

"Deja, I just want to say you look beautiful tonight and I apologize for how stupid I've been acting. Happy birthday." He looked at Danielle and signaled for her to start the song. "May I please have this dance?"

H.E.R.'s *"Every Kind Of Way"* began to play through the speakers and the room became filled with audible 'oohs and aws. Deja blushed and nodded. She walked toward him and wrapped her arms around his neck. Kurt wrapped his arms around her waist pulling her into him as they began to dance. This was, in Deja's mind, the best present she could receive tonight. Jason watched with contempt.

"That fool is so corny," he scoffed.

"Yeah, but he gets results," Rick replied.

As they danced Deja gazed in his eyes. "I'm sorry for everything I did."

"You don't need to apologize. I do. I acted like an idiot. Your past is your past."

Deja tilted her head into him and kissed his lips which garnered even more 'oohs and ah's from the crowd around them. A few other couples joined them dancing together.

Seeing her little sister happy again made Danielle smile. She hoped that her sister could find the happiness with a man who eluded her for so long. As she watched them she didn't realize someone was watching her.

"They certainly make a cute couple don't they?"

Danielle turned and saw Rick behind her. She didn't even realize he was there until now. He stood before her, as handsome as ever. The last man she wanted to see but in a confusing way the only man she wanted to be with. A rush of feelings came over her.

Love.

Lust.

Pain.

Disappointment.

"Yeah, they do. That's what it looks like when a man isn't afraid of a relationship."

Rick took the barb. "You know I'm not the same immature kid I was six years ago."

"Then what are you now?"

"Listen Dani." He exhaled. "I know you're still upset with me and you have every reason to be."

"Well at least we can agree on that."

"Here we go again." Rick rolled his eyes.

"What the hell is that supposed to mean?" Danielle barked.

"It means I'm sick of you throwing the past in my face."

"You broke my fucking heart!"

"Yeah I did and I'm sorry. I was a dumb kid who didn't know what he had in front of him. I fucked up, but that was then this is now. You can't tell me you don't love me. Because I still love you and you still love me."

Danielle stared at him in shock. She didn't know how to respond. He was right. No matter how hard she tried to deny it, she still was in love with him. But there was still a side that didn't want to give in. Everybody at the party caught wind of their argument.

"You wish!" She turned and quickly walked away. She headed to the den away from the party goers. Rick followed her.

"You kissed me."

She turned and faced him. "I was drunk."

"You drove to my house and you kissed me. I didn't force you."

"So what? I was fucked up! And I did something stupid."

"You said you couldn't get me out of your mind. You said I was the reason things went bad between you and Ken. Right?"

A tear streamed down her face. "Do you understand what you did to me? I loved you so much, Rick, and you hurt me."

For the first time, Rick could see the pain he caused. He hated himself.

"And I will never hurt you again." He gently wiped the tear from her face.

He leaned in and kissed her and for the first time in years Danielle let go of the pain she felt. Their passion took over. Kiss after kiss they exchanged. No more holding back. No more denying what was there.

"I love you," she whispered.

"I never stopped," Rick confirmed.

They kissed again. They were so caught up in their passion that they didn't even notice a certain somebody watching them.

"About time you two stop playing."

They both turned and saw Jason looking at them grinning. Rick smiled but Danielle was less than thrilled that he saw them. In her mind he was part of the reason things went wrong in the first place.

"Please don't stop for me." Jason turned around. "Carry on."

"Great." Danielle looked at Rick. "He's the last person I wanted to know about us."

"Don't worry about him. This is all about me and you." He kissed her again.

A New Look

The barbershop has always been known as the black man's country club. A place where brothers can come together, talk sports, music, women, and any other thing under the sun. That was normal. What was unusual to Mike was seeing so many women getting their hair done on the other side of the shop. But he figured it must be working for them because the shop was packed with customers of both sexes. Mike went inside and had a seat.

One of the barbers spotted him. "You need a cut?"

"I'm here for him. The owner." He pointed at the barber three chairs down.

Darnell looked up. He was a little shocked to see Mike in his shop asking for him for a cut. The last time they saw each other was a few days ago at Deja's birthday party. After the shit he caused between him and Starr he was lucky he didn't knock him out. Darnell nodded and finished cutting the customer in his chair. Ten minutes later he signaled to Mike he was ready. He took a seat in the chair and the two alpha males stared at each other in the mirror.

"So how do you want it?" Darnell asked.

"Bald fade."

"And the beard?"

"Just line it up."

Darnell nodded and turned on his clippers. Mike knew he was taking a big risk having Darnell cut his hair. There was no telling what he would do to his hairline but Mike figured the best way to get Darnell to believe what he was about to say was to give him some power. Darnell began to cut his hair and a few moments of silence passed between them.

"So I guess you're wondering why I'm here." Mike

spoke up, breaking the tension.

Darnell turned the chair to the side. "The thought had crossed my mind."

"You gotta understand I love my sister. I won't let anybody hurt her."

"Then we both got something in common after all."

"So why didn't you tell her about your past?"

Darnell sighed. "I was going to but somebody didn't allow me the opportunity to do it first."

"You could have."

"I know man." He exhaled. "Listen, I wanted Starr to get to know me first. The man I am today. Then I was going to tell her about my past. Look I get it, I have two sisters of my own and if a guy ever disrespected either of them I'd gladly take their head off. But I trust them enough to make their own decisions."

"I know. That's why I'm here."

"What do you mean?"

Mike looked at Darnell's reflection in the mirror. "As much as I hate to admit it, I see the way she looks at you. The way you both looked at each other. I think I made a mistake and I wanna fix it."

Darnell sensed Mike's sincerity and went back to cutting his hair. Fifteen minutes later he finished his work and handed Mike a hand held mirror. Mike studied his hair cut in the mirror and was amazed.

"Damn, I think this is the best cut I've ever gotten."

Darnell smiled. "That's what I do."

"You know for a minute there I thought you were gonna jack my hair up." Mike laughed sheepishly.

"Now that would be wrong. What kind of barber would I be if I let my personal beef affect my job? I mean I would have to be some kind of douchebag to sabotage another man like that. A real asshole if you ask me. A low down dirty bitchass fool. Right?"

Darnell glared at Mike through the mirror.

Mike forced a smile. "Uhuh… Yeah. So, here's what I have in mind."

~~~

UNION CITY - MIKE & KIMA'S HOUSE

Starr pulled up in the driveway of her brother's house. The only reason she was there was because Kima asked her to come by to talk about planning Kennedy's sixth birthday party next month. If she saw Mike it would be like he wasn't even there. She was still pissed that he once again stuck his damn nose in her love life. Seeing Darnell the other night at Deja's party was hard. She couldn't deny how he made her feel inside.

Kima answered the front door. "Hey, I'm glad you came over."

"Well you made it sound like life or death," she joked as she walked inside. "It's just a birthday party for a six year old not a sweet sixteen."

"It might as well be, your niece is a little diva in training."

"Well I think I have a few ideas." Starr sat on the couch.

"That's why I got you here." Kima looked at her phone. "Excuse me for a minute I gotta make a call real quick."

"Okay."

Kima left and Starr relaxed on the couch. She pulled out her phone, and started checking her messages.

"Hey sis." Mike walked into the living room.

Starr glanced up at her brother, rolled her eyes, and went back to her phone. Mike fully expected her to ignore him.

"I know why you're upset with me. I went way too far."

Starr looked up at him surprised at his

acknowledgement but not convinced of his sincerity. She went back to her phone.

"I know it's hard for you to believe anything I say to you but I think maybe you'll listen to him instead."

Darnell and Kima walked in from the kitchen and Starr was shocked.

She stood up. "So this why you wanted me to come over so badly?"

Kima nodded. "Yeah, and I really do need your help planning Kennedy's party."

She sighed. "My rate just went up."

"Whatever, just listen to him, Starr." Kima took Mike's hand and they left the living room.

She and Darnell both stared at one another. She could feel her heart beating in her chest. He looked so damn good to her. His muscular body, smooth cocoa brown skin and handsome face were making her weak. But she forced herself to remain calm and remembered that he lied to her.

Darnell was just as anxious as she was. He took in each of her lovely curves. He knew her body well. All five of his sense yearned to hear, see, touch, smell, and taste her again. He knew that this was going to be his only chance to tell his truth.

"So what do you want?" She looked at him sternly.

"When we met, I wanted you to get to know the man I am today. Not the dumb kid I was ten years ago. Besides, I don't think saying, 'Hello my name is Darnell and I'm a convicted felon' would have went over well with you."

She folded her arms. "Okay but you could've tried."

"You're right. I would've. I just didn't want to rush and do it."

"So what happened?"

"It's not that much to tell really. When I was eighteen growing up in Jackson, Mississippi I thought was a real D-boy. I was doing whatever I thought I had to do to get money." He looked at Starr. "You gotta understand, we didn't have much growing up … single mother raising three kids on a fixed income don't leave much left over so I took upon myself to take care of myself and my sisters."

"So what went wrong?"

"The usual. I was making a little money doing the most. Then I got pulled over and got caught with a lot weed under my seat."

"You were just selling weed?"

"Yeah, what did you think I was selling?"

"Nothing, finish the story."

"I had just turned eighteen and the judge was an asshole. He gave me three years and I thought my life was over; but looking back at it now, it was probably the best thing to happen to me. It was a real wake up call. I took advantage of the programs inside and keep my ass out of trouble. I ended up getting out a year early and was lucky to have some family that wanted to see me succeed."

Darnell moved toward Starr and took her hands.

"You're right, I should have told you this sooner but I guess a part of me was ashamed to share that with you. But what's worse than being embarrassed is losing you. I just want another chance."

Her eyes lit up. "You do?"

"Yes. Do you forgive me?"

She leaned in and kissed him. "I'm thinking about it." Darnell kissed her again.

A few minutes later, Starr found her brother in the backyard watching his daughters play. She watched him watching over her nieces and saw their father in him. Sure he was an overbearing fool but he loved her.

"Hey bruh."

Mike looked at her. "Hey."

"Thank you, for doing this."

"It was the least I could do. So is everything okay with you two?"

"Yeah, we're good."

"Great. I'm sorry I got in your business. I promise it won't happen again. I just want you to be happy."

"Darnell makes me happy, Mike. Dad would've liked him too." Starr grinned. "Oh and Mike, If you ever interfere in my love life again, I'll tell Kima about what really happened to Snuffles." Mike's eyes widened like saucers. "Damn shame what happened to that cat."

He stared at her. "How do you know about that?"

"There was white fluff all over the yard. You're lucky I covered for you. But hey, lawn mower accidents happen right?"

"Please don't tell her, seriously. I don't need them kind of problems in my life. Besides that damn cat really was evil."

She hugged him. "I love you, bro."

"I love you, too."

The Worst

After nearly a month in the hospital, Ms. Sharon was finally cleared to go home and she couldn't have been happier. Even though she wasn't hundred percent she was well enough to dress and feed herself. She was sick of being in a hospital room and even more annoyed with the nightly blood draws from the nurses she referred to as vampires. Not to mention the ungodly amount of new pills she had to take daily was maddening.

As soon as the doctor said she could go home she called Rick and told him to be at the hospital ten o'clock sharp so she wasn't surprised when he walked in her room a few minutes before. But what was a surprise was he walked in with Danielle and they were actually talking and laughing with each other.

"Good morning, Ms. Sharon." Danielle greeted with a smile.

"Hey darling."

"Hey mom, you ready to blow this joint?"

"Don't say 'blowing joints' to your mom." Danielle playfully swatted at him. "That just sounds so inappropriate."

Rick looked at her. "What? It's not like I'm passing her a blunt when I'm saying it."

She shook her head. "Don't be so literal. It just sounds wrong."

"It's a figure of speech." He shrugged his shoulders. "It's weird."

"You're weird."

She spiritedly smacked his arm. "Shut up."

"Well aren't you two in good spirits."

Rick gave his mother a kiss on her cheek. "And why

216

wouldn't we be? My momma is going home!"

"Ms. Sharon, that's the best news we've heard in a very long time."

Danielle picked up the bag that was in the chair then stood next to Rick in front of his mother. She slightly leaned into him as she stood and Sharon grinned seeing the obvious body language between them.

"Mom, I stopped at the nurse's station and let them know we're here to take you home so she should be here with the wheelchair any minute."

"Good." She paused and looked at them. "So are you two going to tell me what's going on between the both of you?"

Danielle couldn't fight the grin that spread across her face. "What do you mean, Ms. Sharon?"

"Don't play dumb, sweetheart. You're not very good at it. Are you two back together?"

They both looked at each other and smiled.

"Yeah mom, I guess we are."

Sharon smiled. "Well thank God for small miracles. You two have wasted enough time apart!"

They both laughed. "We just had to smooth over a few things." Danielle looked into Rick's eyes. "But I think we're on the same page now."

"Yeah, we are."

"Good because I am way overdue for some grandbabies."

Rick shook his head. "Mom, can we please get you home before we start talking about reproducing?"

"I agree." Danielle giggled. "We haven't even gone out on a first official date yet."

"You're right. May I take you out tonight, Ms. Queen?"

"Of course," she responded. "Better yet, how about I cook a meal for us tonight at my place?"

An apprehensive expression crossed Rick's face. As

much as he loved her, he knew cooking wasn't her strong suit. "Cook? You wanna cook for me? Ahh, you sure you don't wanna just hang out tonight? There are a few movies out I think that's …"

"Don't be silly! I'm gonna cook you a fabulous home cooked meal. I bet you haven't had a decent meal in years and I have a recipe I've been dying to try out."

"Oh, you have huh? Great … I can't wait."

Sharon smiled. "Well, as long as it all leads to some grandbabies for me, I'm all for it."

Rick and Danielle laughed.

"Wow, well we will be sure to get right on that mom." He shook his head. "Talk about inappropriate."

~~~

ATLANTA - DANIELLE'S CONDO

Danielle looked over her reflection in the full length mirror. She decided to wear a black lace blouse with a pair of skin tight black leggings. Deja was right; she could be sinfully sexy when she wanted to be. She wanted to show Rick what he had been missing all these years. She wore her hair down and knew he liked it when she did. She wondered if he still liked all the things he did before or if the things that made him call off their wedding were still there as well?

She heard her doorbell ring and she answered the door. Rick's eyes lit up when he saw her. Danielle was naturally beautiful so that was no surprise to him but it had been years since he seen her purposely looking sexy. She could tell by the look on his face that Rick liked what he saw.

He smiled. "Hey."

"Hello."

Rick kissed her and walked inside. The smell of something good cooking was another surprise for him. Rick made himself comfortable on the couch.

"I'll have dinner out for us in just a second."

"Okay."

He looked around her stylishly decorated condo. The last time he was there, the night of Deja's party, he didn't get a chance to take in how elegant her place was. It was a style she always had even back when they dated in college. You would have sworn Martha Stewart decorated her room back then too. A few minutes Danielle returned from the kitchen and joined him on the couch.

"Whatever it is you're cooking in there smells good."

"Smells better than how I used to cook back in the day huh," she quipped.

"What? Nah ..."

Danielle chuckled. "It's okay, Rick. I know my cooking was pretty bad back then. You don't have to lie and spare my feelings anymore. I know that's why you didn't want me to cook for you tonight."

He grinned. "Was I that obvious?"

"Yes, but I loved that you did it anyway."

"So how did you improve?"

"For one, I was honest with myself and then I spent a lot of time with Ms. Sharon learning a thing or two."

"Mom always said she was going to teach you a few things. I'm glad you took her up on her offer."

She gazed in his eyes. "I am too."

They kissed each other again. A bell went off in the kitchen and Danielle got up from the couch.

"Come have a seat in the dining room. I'll bring out dinner."

Rick got up, and watched her ass as she went back into the kitchen. He shook his head imagining all the things he was going to do to her tonight. It had been too long since he touched her in all the places he knew she liked. He sat down at the dining room table already set for two. Minutes later, Danielle returned with two covered plates on a tray and placed one in front of Rick. She uncovered the plate and he saw a perfectly cooked rack of lamb. He was blown away by it.

He looked up at her. "You did this?"

She grinned. "Of course I did."

"Wow."

They both enjoyed the meal, conversation, and stole glances exchanging lustful intensions. After they finished, they returned to the couch.

Danielle leaned against Rick's arm and they entwined fingers. "You know," she paused to gather her thoughts, "I've been thinking, the last time we were together things went bad because we weren't honest with each other. I think this time around we should make that a priority."

"I thought that was a given with any relationship?"

"Yes it is but I just want us to start off in a clear direction."

"I agree." Rick kissed Danielle's forehead.

"So what have you been doing with your life for the past six years?"

"Just living life.

"Must have been exciting traveling with the Lakers and working with the players."

"Yeah, good times." Rick nodded. "I love working with them."

Danielle gave a sly smile. "So did you ever meet anybody out there? Somebody special?"

"No, nobody special. Just dated."

"The life of a bachelor huh?" She unhooked her fingers from his, sat up and faced him.

"I guess. Women in LA. can be fickle."

"Fickle? In what way?"

"Well, everybody is trying to get noticed. Wanting to be a movie star or trying to hook up with a baller. Not too many are looking for a long term relationship."

"Well, there are a lot of pretty woman out there to choose from."

"Yeah," Rick admitted. "You can't throw a rock

without hitting one."

"I'm sure." She stared at him. "So, how many?"

He looked at her oddly. "How many what?"

"Women. How many have you thrown rocks at?" She clarified.

"You're serious?" He looked at her, not believing what she asked.

She continued to stare, waiting for an answer.

"I didn't keep count."

"Wow, that many." She shook her head. "Why am I not surprised?"

"Why would you even ask me that?"

"Why shouldn't I? Figures you would become a man whore working in the NBA."

"Whoa, whoa, whoa, why I gotta be a man whore? Because I didn't keep track of how many women I slept with? I didn't ask you for a body count."

"Two," she told him dryly.

Rick looked at her surprised. "Two? Just two, in six years? Wow. Really?"

"Yes really; Alonzo Hall and Chauncey Bryant. Both I were in relationships with. So just tell me do you even remember the name of the last woman you slept with?"

"Of course I do! This crazy married chick named Carla."

"Married?" Danielle frowned. "You're sleeping with married women now?"

"Whoa, wait a minute, I didn't know she was married at the time. We just hooked up!"

"Oh that makes it even better!" She folded her arms across her chest.

"Oh okay, so I guess you weren't gonna make Ken number three on your list the night you showed up drunk at my place huh?"

If looks could kill, Rick would have been dead. They both sat in silence for a moment both feeling a bit irritated with the other. This is why Rick generally avoided telling the truth on first dates. No good ever came from it.

"Dani, whatever we did before this moment is in the past. He took her hand again. "I don't want it to affect what we have now."

"Yeah, you're right," she admitted. "I shouldn't have gone there."

"It's cool." The corners of his lips turned upward. "But there are other places we can go."

He leaned in and gently kissed her. Danielle reciprocated his passion. Rick's hand caressed her leg but before things could get more intense, she pulled away abruptly.

"We can't do this. It's too soon."

"But we have, plenty of times in the past."

"That was then, this is now."

He touched her thigh. "Yeah but ..."

"We're not having sex tonight." She removed his hand.

"Really? Oh, you're serious. No sex at all?"

"Nope."

"What if I just put the tip in?"

She gave him the side eye. "I don't know where your 'tip' has been for the last six years."

"That was a joke, Dani."

"I'm not laughing." She stood up. "Is getting between my legs the only thing on your mind tonight?"

"Oh c'mon! Seriously! Why can't you just let go and live in the moment?"

"Maybe because I like to think ahead and not make a mistake!"

"Mistake?" Rick got up. "You wanna know why things didn't work between us before? Because you're a control freak!"

She frowned. "What!"

"Yeah, like the same way you've tried to control this

whole night! The way you insisted on cooking dinner, then the whole let's be completely honest and make me confess how many woman I've banged over the years! Now we gotta wait because it's too soon? Dani, I love you but I'm not going to play this game with you anymore." He turned and headed toward the door. "Call me when you wanna act like a grown up."

Danielle was stunned by Rick's rant and a little lost for words but she damn sure wasn't going to let him have the last one. "Don't hold your breath, asshole!"

Rick left and Danielle stood in the center of her living room speechless. She couldn't help but think he had some fucking nerve. Once again a man had left her horny and pissed off.

"Fuck my life!"

The Jerk

Her romantic relationships over the years may have been rocky but the one thing Danielle was always good at was her job. Over the past few years she became a successful defense attorney. She sat at her desk reviewing case files trying to put her personal life out of her mind. Normally focusing on work would do the trick but not today. Rick stayed on her mind.

After her fight with him two nights ago she decided that getting back together was a mistake. *Why did I ever think we could work?* The more she tried not to think about him the more she did. Focusing on work was becoming impossible. Her office phone rang and saw it was the front desk.

She answered. "Yes LaShune?"

"Your three o'clock is here. In conference room B."

"Thanks." She hung up.

Danielle sighed, got up from her chair, and exited the office. It was time to get focused and do what she does best—help people. She walked down the hallway, stopped in front of the conference room and adjusted her blouse before she walked inside. Her client was seated in a chair with his back facing her.

"Hello Mr. Henderson. How can I help you today?"

He spun around in his chair. "You can help me help you."

"Jason," Danielle barked, "what the hell do you think you're doing?"

"I'm just here to talk."

"We don't have anything to talk about. How dare you come to my job with this foolishness!" She angrily stomped toward him. "I've tolerated your rude ass for years out of respect but coming here is too much!"

Jason expected the outburst and tried not to smile. He always liked her spunk. "I'm here to talk about you and Rick."

"You're the absolute last person I ever want to talk to about that."

"I know we've never gotten along but the one thing we do have in common is Rick. It's about time you two stop playing games and get it together."

"Did he send you here?" She put her hands on her hips. "Is he paying you to do this?"

"Paying me? He should be!" Jason leaned back confidently in the chair. "Rick doesn't know I'm here. I decided I'd better be the voice of reason around here."

"Voice of reason? From you?" She folded her arms. "You've never liked me or my relationship with him! You're the fucking reason why we didn't get married in the first place!"

"Is that what you think? I'm the reason? You really believe that?"

"That's what I know."

"And you call yourself a lawyer." He shook his head. "I expected more from you."

"Admit it, you were the one putting all those doubts in his head about marrying me back then. You didn't want lose your sidekick! You just wanted him to become a man whore like you. Well congratulations, Rick has graduated summa cum whore of his class! Sleeping with married women and god knows what else he's been doing over the years."

"Whoa, whoa, whoa." Jason stood up. "Rick banged a married chick? That sly dog ain't tell me about that shit! I'ma have to have a word with him about that."

Danielle grunted in disgust.

"Look, your relationship failed back then for the same reason it backfired now. Because you love to control everything and everybody around you."

"Screw you."

"That's the real truth. Rick is my best friend, I know him and I knew he wasn't ready for marriage back then. He barely knew what he really wanted in life at that point. If you two would've gotten married it would've ended in divorce. We both know that."

Danielle knew that was the truth. As much as she hated to admit it she always knew that Rick wasn't one hundred percent ready to get married. She just thought if she gave him a little push that maybe he would see that they were meant to be. That was a truth she denied to herself for years. It was just easier to hate Rick and blame Jason than admit to her own fault in their demise.

She took a breath. "So why are you here now? I'm a control freak right? You should be happy we're not together."

"I'm not happy seeing my best friend miserable. In case you didn't know Dani, Rick loves your over the top ass."

She stared at Jason, speechless.

"For the past two days Rick has been depressed as hell. I can't shake him out of it and I tried everything, basketball, liquor, hookers." A shit eating grin spread across his face.

"Fuck you, Jason!"

"I'm just playing." He laughed, knowing he got under her skin. "Listen, Rick wasn't sure about what he wanted back then but he knows what he wants now and that's you. You just have to get out your own way and let that man love you."

Danielle thought about what Jason was saying and simmered down. "He still wants to be with me?"

"Of course he does. He needs you."

She was quiet for a moment as she pondered Jason's words. She realized this time she was the problem in their relationship and it was up to her to fix it.

She let her guard down. "I never wanted to admit it but Rick is lucky to have a best friend like you."

"I've been telling you that for years."

"Well, you better get your shit together too." She pointed at him.

"About what?"

Dani folded her arms. "My sister."

"Oh, so you know about that huh?"

"I know enough and you were a dick for doing what you did. But that tells me for you to do that you must care about her more than you're letting on. She was your friend before anything else but what you did was selfish. If there's one thing I know about you is that you value friendship."

"So both of the Queen sisters hate me now? Nice," he huffed.

"I don't hate you, Jason."

"Really?"

"I wasn't fond of you but I honestly never hated you … completely."

"And Deja?"

"Oh she hates your ass. I suggest you go fix it."

~~~

ATLANTA - DEJA'S APARTMENT

"I missed you so much," Kurt whispered in Deja's ear.

She smiled. "You don't have to miss me anymore."

The two were naked in her bed. Kurt spooned behind her. He had been, for more or less, living at Deja's apartment for the last couple of days. Ever since her birthday party, they had been making up for lost time. Most of that time was in bed making love. The dating rules she normally had in play in the past had no place in the relationship with Kurt.

"Are you hungry," she asked. "I can make something for us."

"That's okay, I got something I wanna eat right here." His head disappeared underneath the covers. Deja rolled on her back as her legs spread apart.

227

"Oh, ahhhhh …"

An hour later, Kurt was in the kitchen making Deja an egg sandwich while she sat at the table with a smile on her face. This was unlike any relationship she had ever had before and she liked it. The doorbell chimed and she headed toward the door. When she looked through the peephole, she frowned, seeing who it was.

"What the hell are you doing here," she snapped opening the door.

Jason grinned seeing her in her robe looking sexy as hell. "I come in peace." He held up his hands. "I just wanted to say something to you."

A shirtless Kurt walked up behind Deja. "Whatever you got to say you can say it to both of us."

Deja sneered and put her arm around Kurt's toned waist.

"True. It's good to see you two back together again, all happy and after sex glowing and shit."

"You got five seconds to say what you gotta say," Deja warned.

"Listen, I just want to apologize for what I did. It was childish and selfish; especially to you, Deja. Long before anything happened between us we were friends. And I admit I felt some type of way when I found out about you two. But that's no excuse for being a dick. Even though I'm a dick most of time but I was really big dick to you." Deja's eyes bucked and Kurt looked like he was about to kick his ass. "Pause, that came out wrong. It sounded much better in my head before I said that. Anyway, I'm sorry."

Deja couldn't fight the smile on her face. "You're a jerk. Apology accepted."

"Jason, we've never been the best of friends, so I see no need for us to start now." Kurt wrapped his arms around Deja.

Jason nodded. "I agree. Anyway, y'all crazy kids get

back to doing all those nasty freaky things."

"Goodbye Jason." Deja closed the door in his face.

With a tilted grin, he left, and headed toward his car. His phone buzzed and he saw a text message from an unknown number.

⇨ HELLO JASON, I KNOW IT'S BEEN A LONG TIME BUT I'M IN TOWN AND I NEED TO SEE YOU. I'M AT THE W. PLEASE COME. SELENA.

"Selena?"

Reading that text froze him in his tracks. It had been years since he heard from her. Memories he tried to forget flooded his memory like they were yesterday. A hedonistic lifestyle with a woman he loved played back in his mind like old VHS tapes. He smiled remembering the good times they had. Many nights of good food, expensive wine, and explicit sex ran through his mind. Then that painful day in the lobby of the W came back to him as well. Pain he had pushed away was still there. It had never really gone away. He considered deleting the text and ignoring her but his heart wouldn't allow him to do that. He still wanted answers as to why she left him. If there ever was a woman he wished to have a second chance with, Selena was the one.

Lose Control

Dark clouds rolled in over Atlanta a little after five o'clock in the afternoon like the weather man predicted and down came the rain. Rick just checked in on his mother who was sound asleep in her room. Since her return home, Rick noticed that she was a bit slower than before. She was able to move around but she need to take breaks more often than not. Her heart was weak but her spirit was strong.

Outside of his mother's health, Danielle stayed on his mind. He wanted to be with her but he refused to let her control every aspect of their relationship like she did before. As much he loved her he had to draw the line somewhere. Even so, that didn't stop his heart from aching. After all these years of wanting a second chance to be with her it was a damn shame to see nothing had changed.

Rick decided it was time for a change in his life, with or without the woman he loved. Moving back to Atlanta was the right thing especially now that his mother needed him now more than ever. For the past month Rick had been living comfortably off his savings. He didn't want to exhaust those funds so he decided to take the sports medicine position with the Atlanta Hawks. He already broke the lease on his apartment in LA and would fly back in a few days to get the rest of his things.

The rain was coming down hard outside. Thunder rattled the walls. Most of the lights in the house were off except for a hallway light making the house dimly lit. Rick was cozy sitting on the couch looking for apartments on his tablet. He wanted to find a spot close to his mother's house maybe in Midtown. He always loved being in the heart of Atlanta. The doorbell rang and Rick glanced up at the door. He wondered who was out in the middle of this god awful weather as he got up and walked to the door. He looked out the peephole and couldn't believe it.

He opened the door. "Hey."

She was soaked from the rain. "Hi."

Rick quickly ushered her inside. "You're drenched."

"I forgot my umbrella."

They stared at each other for a moment. So many things being expressed in a moment without a word being said. They both didn't know quite where to begin.

"I needed to see you."

He looked on.

"You were right. I am a control freak."

Rick didn't know how to respond. Danielle had never conceded before.

"I don't know why I am the way I am. I just can't control it. I know it's a flaw and don't know if I will ever be to fix it but." She stared into his eyes. "I just know that, I don't wanna control you."

Rick walked toward her and pulled her raincoat over her shoulders. It fell to the floor. Rick caressed her face, and gently kissed her. Tongues touched. Passion exploded. All restraint let go. Rick hoisted her up off her feet and carried her to the spare bedroom they both knew so well.

He put her down and a nervous smile spread across her face as he unbuttoned her half soaked blouse. Danielle unbuttoned her pants and pulled them down to the floor. A pair of lacy black panties contained her thickness. Rick took a moment to admire her beautiful physique. She was finer than he remembered. She peeled off her blouse and revealed the matching bra underneath.

She sat back on the queen sized bed behind her as Rick undressed himself. She could tell that he continued to put time in the gym by his sculptured body. He wasn't a muscle bound jock but he was certainly cut in all the right places. First his shirt, then his jeans leaving him in pair of dark blue boxer briefs that left almost nothing to the imagination. A long hard print stretched the fabric. Danielle grinned at the thought of what he would do to her with it.

Rick smiled seeing that look on her face. She unfastened her bra and tossed it to the side. Her breasts were nice and soft. Not to big but a mouthful to enjoy. Rick pulled down his boxers and let his hardness stand tall and ready, a long thick dick that resembled some exotic fruit at the farmers market. His manhood looked more deadly than the silver bullet she kept in her nightstand. Danielle exhaled as Rick went toward her but then he stopped. She looked at him confused.

"What's wrong?"

"I forgot something." He turned and head toward the door. "I'll be right back!"

"Okay."

He exited the room and Danielle sat a little confused. Then she quickly stood up and removed her panties and tossed them near her bra. She caught a glimpse of herself in the mirror and smiled. Sitting up on the bed, she crossed her legs, and Rick returned to the room with a condom in hand. He grinned and ambled toward the bed. Danielle opened her legs and showed him her gateway to heaven. She took his erection in her hand stroked it, caressed it, made it grow harder. A soft growl escaped his lips. Then she took the condom out of his hands, tore it open with her mouth, and rolled it on his hard member. He kissed her lips, her neck, and then her breasts. Sucking each nipple then he slowly pushed himself inside. Danielle gasped feeling him enter her. It had been a while since she felt the real thing. Her warmth surrounded him, his hardness excited her and she welcomed him deep inside. Each stroke brought her pleasure; soft moans escaped her lips, as each kiss was a reminder of what they meant to each other.

She curled her legs around Rick as he moved in and out of her wetness. Fingernails on his back as soft kisses touched her neck. They changed positions with her on top riding his erection. She moved her hips like a stripper doing a nasty dance. She was in control but Rick didn't mind. He was content to let her have her way with him for now. She swayed her hips from left to right; her wetness made a swishing sound. It felt too good to stop. She bounced, wiggled, and jerked her body making Rick hum a sweet song. She breathed heavily through her mouth giving herself the best workout she's had in years.

Soon it was his turn to take control as he entered her from the back. His muscular body pounded her soft round ass and muffled moans in a pillow filled the room. Soft groans and words that made no sense left her lips. She enjoyed his roughness as she glanced back at him. Rick turned her around, laid her on her back, and gazed into her eyes. He made a vow to himself that he wasn't going to lose her again. She smiled as if she was reading his mind. Two lost lovers reconnected both physically, mentally and spiritually once again.

The next morning, Danielle woke up in the arms of the man she loved. She felt exhausted from their hours of love making. She could smell eggs and toast in the air. She almost forgot Rick's mother was there. She cringed at the thought of her hearing their love making last night. Her stomach growled.

"Well that's a familiar sound," Rick said and kissed her neck.

"We didn't exactly eat dinner last night. God, do you think your Mom heard us?"

"Nah, she was all the way upstairs."

She leaned her head back on the pillow. "So what happens next?"

"I don't know but let's just find out together."

She turned and kissed him. Just as their passion started to rise again they heard a knock on the door. Danielle froze in embarrassment.

"Rick?" His mother called out.

"Yeah mom?"

"Breakfast is on the table."

"Okay... thanks."

"And tell Danielle to come get something to eat too."

Rick laughed as she closed her eyes and hid her face in his chest. Sharon walked away with a smile on her face knowing her wish had come true.

Epilogue
A New Situation

THE W HOTEL ATLANTA - MIDTOWN

Jason walked through the lobby of the luxurious W Hotel on his way to meet an old acquaintance he hadn't seen in six years. Jason would never admit it to anyone but Selena Kirby was the one woman that ever really got inside his heart. She was the one woman he would have given anything for and be the man she needed.

Now, after all this time, she contacted him out the blue asking him to meet her at her same place it started. If she wanted to rekindle what they once had Jason was more than willing. Only this time, he would protect his heart. Like many times before, he stood at the door of her oversized suite and knocked. Nervously, he exhaled. Then the door opened and he saw her. Jason thought it was almost impossible for her to look better than she did six years ago but she did.

Selena smiled. "Hello Jason."

"Hey."

He stared at her in awe. It was like déjà vu all over again; only this time, her once Pixie haircut was now shoulder length. She had the same beautiful face and her body had filled out even more. She was a brick house in every sense of the word.

"Well, are you gonna come give me a hug?"

"Oh hell yeah." Jason wrapped his arms around her body and squeezed her tight. He inhaled a familiar sweet vanilla scent that aroused him and she brushed her lips against his neck. The chemistry they once had was still there. If they held onto one another any longer a sexual explosion was going to happen. Selena wisely stepped away from him.

"Come in." She gestured.

Jason strolled into the luxury suite and remembered

236

all the good times they had there. Apparently money was still no object for her. She closed the door behind her.

He turned and looked at her. "I gotta say, I was surprised to hear from you again after the way you left."

"I'm sorry. I didn't handle that the right way but I think it's time for us to reconnect. I have so much I want to tell you."

"Okay, well I'm here."

She nervously rubbed her hands. "Do you want a drink?" She walked by him to the mini bar. "There's a little of everything."

"Yeah, I remember."

He could see how uneasy she was. He had never seen her like this. Something was on her mind so he decided not to push her too fast.

She looked at him and grinned. "Let me see if I remember, Hennessey and Coke?"

He nodded, she made his drink, and brought it to him.

"I like the way you let your bread grow out. It looks good on you."

"Thanks." He drank some then gazed at her. "Everything looks good on you too."

She blushed. "Thank you."

Jason leaned in and kissed her. It was a passionate kiss that took her breath away. It took all her willpower to step away from him. Jason looked into her eyes.

"Why did you leave me? You just left with no warning or nothing. Why?"

"Believe me, I didn't have a choice in the matter." She sighed. "That's a lie. I did have a choice. I just made the wrong choice and I've regretted it every day."

"Why couldn't you just talk me? Maybe I could've helped."

"Not with this. Remember when I told you I had a complicated relationship with my father?" She paused. "He controlled a lot of things in my life back then and didn't approve of us. Once I told him what my intentions were with you, he gave me an ultimatum, and told me if I didn't leave you he would cut me off completely."

He was shocked. "What?"

"I'm sorry, Jason. I wish I was a stronger person back then. There were so many things happening and I was afraid to give up everything I knew. So I choose it over you."

He exhaled and took another swig of his drink.

Jason nodded. "I get it. I was just some guy you met in Atlanta. So what changed now?"

"Everything and you were never just some random guy to me." Selena looked at him nervously. "There's something I need to tell you. Something I should have told you years ago. The reason my father made me leave you."

"Made you?" He looked at her concerned. "What was it?"

"There's someone here I want you to meet." She smiled and looked toward the spare bedroom. "Janice, come here please."

The door opened and the cutest little girl Jason had ever seen emerged from the room. She was dressed in a pretty blue dress like a princess and stood by Selena's side. Jason didn't know how to react. This was the last thing expecting to see. He stared at her face.

Janice waved her hand. "Hi."

"Hi." Jason waved back then looked at Selena. "You have child?"

"Yes, she's five."

He bent down in front of her. "You're the prettiest thing I've ever seen." He looked up at Selena. "Is she mine?"

A tear fell from her eye. "Yes, she is. Her name is Janice Trammell."

Jason deeply exhaled and tears rimmed his eyes as he stared at his daughter's pretty face. Janice reached out and touched his face and wiped away his tears.

"Don't cry, daddy."

Jason smiled and hugged his child. He never thought he could fall in love with anybody so instantly. In his heart he knew that he would do anything to protect her. And just like that Jason had a new situation in his life.

The Cast

Chasity Marie as Deja Queen

LeThomas Lee as Jason Trammell

Tarver Harris as Kurt Bishop

Kiya Jefferson as Danielle "Dani" Queen

Sayyed Shabazz as Rick Westbrook

Tara Johnson as Starr Sales

Ryan Taylor as Darnell Smith

LaToya Thompson as Kima Rowe-Sales

Bakari Holley as Mike Sales

Acknowledgements

In a lot of ways this story is the spiritual sequel to another novel I wrote called Used To Temporary Happiness. But it's not. Let me explain, after I wrote the novel we filmed a small independent film and we casted the characters with actors. When I say we I mean, myself and Lamont Gant at Creative Genius Films who also designed this incredible book cover for me. I mean wow, will ya look at that sucka?! Fabulous! Anywho we casted Chasity, Kiya, Tarver, LeThomas, Sayyed, LaToya, Bakri, Tara, and Ryan for the film. Over the year or so we took to make the film we all got to know each other very well and I always thought to myself, now that I know these folks I would cast them in slightly different roles and have them play off of each other. So when I started writing My Current Situation I had all of these people in my head. As I was writing the personalities of the characters and situations they were in just naturally felt comedic in tone so I just leaned into and said I wanna make y'all laugh. So hopefully you did.

I chose Chasity (Deja), LeThomas (Jason), and Tarver (Kurt) for the cover because I knew how much chemistry they had together and it just popped in every picture they took. Thank you all for bring my vision to life!

My editor, Cynthia Marie, boy did we go in on this one! You are the Yoda to my Skywalker, the Ike to my Tina, the Mister to my Celie, oh my god I think I'm in abusive relationship ... you've been whooping my ass for years... I needed every bit of it. Even when we don't agree I loved that you give me another point of view. Thank you for gracing me with your awesomeness!

To my beautiful wife Sheena, thank you for supporting me in all that I do.

Priscilla V. Sales, Thank you gave me my first break in the industry. I will never forget it.

To every author writing a book independently

without major backing, don't stop. When people ask me how long did it take for me to become an author or how was I able to get my screenplays produced into films I always say, it didn't happen overnight. You have to get used to people telling you no. I remembered keeping every rejection letter just as a reminder of how hard I worked. And looking back, to be honest with myself, my stuff wasn't as good as I thought it was. Those rejections made me work harder and get better at my craft. I'm thankful for it. Follow your heart, listen to those you truly respect, and if they don't want to give you a chance, do it yourself!

See you all in the next book!

Marlon McCaulsky

7/13/2019 – 12:25PM

About the Author

Originally from Brooklyn, NY and was raised in St. Petersburg FL, Marlon McCaulsky is the author of eight novels, including *The Pink Palace, The Pink Palace 2, From Vixen 2 Diva, Used To Temporary Happiness, Born Sinners, Returned, Blush, If I Was your Girlfriend,* and *Romance For The Streets* and contributing co-writer of the screenplays *Returned, Temporary Happiness, No Time For Love,* and *Annulment* for Creative Genius Films. He lives in Atlanta, GA.

www.marlonmccaulsky.com

Made in the USA
Middletown, DE
24 February 2021